Escapade

Charles Owen

Telling Tales: Vol 4

Books by Charles Owen

Novellas:

FIAMMA

CRY CASSANDRA !

Telling Tales:

Vol 1: A CRACK IN THE GLASS

Vol 2: THE MARK OF THE BEAST

Vol 3: MAN OVERBOARD

Vol 4: ESCAPADE

Copyright

CONTENTS

Working Undercover   Page 5

Escapade   Page 16

Fetch !   Page 44

War Games   Page 49

Rapport   Page 66

The Learning Curve   Page 117

About the Author   Page 161

Acknowledgements   Page 164

Working Undercover

'No hard feelings, I trust?' Bill Findlay had heard that I was leaving the Foreign Service and taking early retirement and, at lunchtime on my last day, we went to a pub near Victoria Street for a pie and a couple of pints.

'One or two,' I replied with a chuckle. Findlay was with Special Branch.

'We couldn't let it go on,' he said. 'You do see that, don't you, Philip?'

'And I so nearly got away with it. It was Dudley's last visit when you pulled him in for questioning.'

'Out of how many?'

'About ten, over a period of several months. By that time, I had a complete set of plans. How long did you have him under surveillance?'

'Three weeks. Of course, we knew that he was on our side because whatever it was that the Russian woman passed to him ended up on your desk.'

'So, why did you interfere?'

'It only takes a few moments to hand over a small package. His visits were lasting for an hour, sometimes longer.'

'What a spoilsport you are!'

'It wasn't just that. The police wanted their property back.'

'Dudley was helping you. At least that was what he believed.'

'He told us that and, of course, we released him straight away.'

'You must have found the whole business very puzzling.'

'I am still puzzled, Philip. Suppose you start from the beginning?'

'Well, I had lunch with my brother-in-law in one of those large London clubs.'

'At your invitation?'

'Yes." Dudley had kept most of his hair and his figure and he was a good-looking man. I know some clever stockbrokers but I never credited him with being overburdened with brains. Useful connections, however, combined with an easygoing charm and good looks will still take you a long way in business.

'After lunch we went into the sitting room and had a cup of coffee. "I will never become senior partner, Philip," he said. "But I don't want the job. I don't work very hard. I can take an afternoon off and nobody would miss me. All the same, I reckon that I pull my weight. When Henley Week comes around and then Ascot and Goodwood, I am in charge of the corporate entertaining. It sounds fun but it can be quite exhausting."

'"But, on the whole, the job suits you," I said, "and you appear to be comfortably off."

'"I have more than enough money. The two boys are independent and we have a nice house in Pimlico."

'"And my sister, Jennie?"

'Dudley frowned and poured himself a second cup. "To my mind, she got married too young. I'm partly to blame. It was baby-snatching. She was only just eighteen. I was over thirty."

'"I put you at little more than fifty."

'"Spot on, Philip, and Jennie is not yet forty. It's a big gap. I would like to tell you that I make her happy but it wouldn't be true. I'm sorry to say that we have grown apart. We don't attract each other any longer – at least, not in that sort of way."

'"You would never leave her?"

'"*Of course not*! We are very fond of each other." He sighed. "That said, I admit that we have very few interests in common. She is a good linguist. She can read Thomas Mann or Dostoevsky in the original. Somerset Maugham is as close as I get to culture. As for music, she loves the opera. She dragged me off to see *Eugene Onegin* a few days ago. Three hours of screeching and caterwauling and a heroine who must have weighed fourteen stone. It was unendurable."

'"Your tastes may be very different but both your sons are doing well, I believe. That must give you and Jennie a lot of satisfaction?"

'"It does, but it is sad that we see so little of them. Henry works for a commodity firm in Dubai. William is a director of a hedge fund in Hong Kong."

'"Any girl friends?"

'"They are spoiled for choice but neither of them shows any sign of getting married. Perhaps if we had had daughters…" he shrugged and left the sentence unfinished.

'There was silence between us for a few moments. I could see the question mark in Dudley's eyes. Then he came out with it. "It's always pleasant to meet, Philip, and I have enjoyed my lunch, but I know that you are a busy chap…"

'I smiled. "You have the feeling that this is rather more than a social occasion?"

'He nodded. "I know very little about your work except that you have some sort of hush-hush job at the Foreign Office."

'"You make it sound more mysterious than it is, but you are right. What I wanted to see you about is connected with my work."

'It was Dudley's turn to smile. "I thought as much."

'We retrieved our overcoats. It was a nice autumn day, fine but cold, and the club had a small garden so we sat together on one of the benches. "The situation," I began, "is a little unusual. We need to keep an eye on the comings and goings at the Russian Embassy in London. That's a job for Special Branch and, if there is something that we ought to know, they come to us with it – and, if it is serious, it goes upstairs, so to speak. Special Branch has had tentative approaches from a woman who is employed there as a cipher clerk. Her first name is Tamara. She is in her late thirties, unmarried and unhappy. She asked to be posted back to Moscow but she was turned down."

'"Why was that?"

'"She says that her employers do not trust her. They suspect that she is out of sympathy with

the Communist system and the regime."

'"And is she?"

'"Yes."

'"How do you know that?"

'"We exchange messages in what we term 'dead letter boxes'. We might leave a note in a hole in a tree in the park. She might tape her reply to the underneath of a stone. Sometimes we communicate by means of a message hidden in a toy sailing boat, she on one side of the Round Pond, one of our spooks on the other."

'Dudley scratched his head. "It's all very interesting, Philip, but why are you telling me this?"

'"I'm coming to that. We believe that Tamara is keen to defect. But the United Kingdom does not welcome all would-be defectors. There is no point in upsetting our relationship with the Russians just for the sake of it. Everything depends on what these people bring with them."

'"What is Tamara offering?"

'"She claims that she is in possession of high-grade material."

'"Do you believe her?"

'"We cannot take that on trust. We have to pass it to our experts to look at."

'"That's a job for your department."

'"We share our findings with the boffins at the Ministry of Defence. But first we have to obtain the material. Members of our security services are known to the Russians. If she is seen with one of them, she would be arrested and her future, if she had one, would be very grim."

'"Are you saying that she is being watched?"

'"Yes, in the sense that security is very tight at the Embassy. She would have to smuggle the material out of the building. She might not be able to pass more than small pieces of information at any one time. It could be a month or two before we had enough information to be able to assess Tamara's potential value to the West."

'"Where is this taking us, Philip?"

'"We want you to make contact with her."

'"*Why me – of all people!* You must realise that I have no qualifications for this sort of hole-in-the-corner business?"'

'"You have one huge advantage over any conceivable alternative."'

'Dudley's eyebrows shot up. "I have? *Philip, you astonish me!*"'

'"She saw you at the opera house three evenings ago. She said that you were the best-looking man that she had ever set eyes on."'

'"*She said that!* Is that one of the qualifications for this assignment?"'

'"It might be. At least, it would get you off to a good start. But it is not the main one. She wants someone that she feels she can trust. Someone kind, upright, a bit old-fashioned, perhaps. Not a spook or a spy or a part of the East Bloc–West Bloc Punch and Judy show. She has a horror of all that. I believe that you would be the perfect intermediary. 'Find me someone like that handsome gentleman I saw in Row K.' That's what she wrote in her last message."'

'"Did she say where she was sitting the evening that she saw me?"'

'"She was exactly behind you but two rows back."'

'"So that is how she knew my seat number."'

'"She mentioned that there was an empty seat next to you during the first interval."'

'"Jennie went to get an ice cream."'

'"Tamara said that you were reading the libretto. She was very impressed."'

'"Jennie left the libretto on her chair. I picked it up and used it as a shield while I did the *Evening Standard* crossword."'

'I laughed. "Well, you don't have to tell Tamara that."

'"What is our next move?"

'"You sound interested."

'"I am interested."

'"Then I will tell her that I have traced you through the box office and that you are going to help."

'"What does she look like?"

'"She is most attractive. An oval face, high cheekbones, cornflower-blue eyes, long blonde hair."

'Dudley leaned forward over the table and fixed me in the eyes. "You are really serious about this, Philip?"

'"Deadly serious."

'"For King and Country, that sort of thing?"

'"Exactly that."

'"Would Jennie have to be told?"

'"*Certainly not*! You are working undercover. Your relationship with Tamara will be on a strictly professional basis."

'"How do I meet her?"

'"There is an old barge anchored on the south side of the Thames opposite Chelsea Reach. The River Police use it for surveillance work but they don't need it for a couple of months."

'"I cannot let this interfere with my City job, Philip."

'"It need not. You must make contact with her every other Thursday, but long, light evenings would not be helpful. The clocks go back at the weekend. Thursday next week is your first day. Take the Underground to Sloane Square and then the bus that crosses Battersea Bridge.

Vary your route each time. Make sure you are not followed."

"'I know the area. There are some steps that lead from the bridge down to the river."

"'That is right. Walk along the embankment until you come to the barge. There is only one moored there. The light will be fading. Time your journey so that you arrive at exactly six o'clock in the evening. Cross the gangway and tap three times on the door – one light tap and two heavier ones. Wait until you hear her reply with one heavy tap."

"'Morse code?"

"'Correct. D for Dudley. T for Tamara."

"'Supposing she is late?"

"'She won't be. She gets in to work very early and leaves the Embassy at four."

"'Anything else"

"'Take a pencil torch."

"'Are there no lights inside?"

"'There are heavy curtains and the windows may be blacked out. Not a glimmer of light can be permitted to show on the outside. That is of the first importance. The barge is meant to be unoccupied."

"'Do the River Police know about this?"

"'Yes. But they make the rules and we have to abide by them."

"'How good is her English?"

"'Very rudimentary. But you will not be holding long conversations. Each time you visit, she will hand you a small package. Don't open it. Take it home and put it in your safe overnight. Then hand it in to commissionaire in Charles II Street on your way to the office on the Friday morning. He will bring it straight to me.""'

Bill Findlay drained his glass. 'What are we meant to do about Tamara?'

'You don't need to worry about her. She has gone back to Russia.'

'Voluntarily?'

'I doubt it.'

'You are a ruthless so-and-so, Philip. You make use of this woman. She runs great risks on your behalf and then you throw her to the wolves.'

***

I left the office promptly after work and walked to Piccadilly. Jennie and I had agreed to meet at Fortnum's for a cup of tea. She looked radiant. There wasn't a hint of grey in her glossy brown hair and her hazel eyes were full of barely suppressed laughter.

'You have been given the sack and so have I,' she said, giggling.

'There is a great deal of difference between retiring early on a full pension and being fired,' I replied with mock severity. 'Which of you has been given the heave-ho?'

'Tamara.' She reached under the table and handed me a small parcel. 'One blonde wig. One pair of eau-de-Nil silk pyjamas. You had better have them, Philip. It would never do if Dudley found them in the house.'

'What about the contact lenses?'

'I have thrown them away.'

'And the aids and accessories?'

'The sex toys, you mean? I have kept some of the more outlandish ones. I might need them again.'

'Jennie, you have become quite shameless. Did Dudley never suspect you?'

'Never. The hammer and sickle was the clincher.'

'What are you talking about?'

'It was a tattoo. Only a temporary one.'

'Thank heavens for that.'

'You just press it on like one of those transfers. Mine was luminous. It shone in the dark.'

'Where did you wear that?'

'Where do you think? The hammer on one side; the sickle on the other.'

'*Outrageous!* Did Dudley learn any Russian – among other things?'

'We didn't talk very much. I had to look up one or two of the words.'

'You make it sound fascinating. Why did he dump you?'

Jennie yawned. 'He was tired of me.'

'I don't believe it.'

'Well, he may have been just plain tired. Anyway, his work was finished. He went back to his cosy wife.'

'Will he be nicer to you now?'

'Of course. He won't be able to resist.' She sighed happily. 'I learned so much from Tamara.'

'What sort of things – or shouldn't I ask?'

'Tamara taught me that a woman's bedroom is a stage. She can be the leading lady in her own play.'

When I got home, I pieced together the sections of the plan that I had given Tamara and which had come back to me by way of Dudley. It was the blueprint for a new service lift in one of Moscow's Underground stations. I will put it in a little frame and keep it as a memento. I wonder where Jennie will hide her hammer and sickle.

Escapade

Beyond the college spires the sky was lightening. A punt appeared out of the mist and drifted past like an image from a dream. Close to a weeping willow, a group of undergraduates in evening dress were reclining on the riverbank, oblivious of the heavy dew which had soaked the grass. White ties were untied and waistcoats unbuttoned; the girls had kicked off their shoes.

Hugo tugged gently at a strand of long chestnut hair. 'Finals are over. The dance is over. To all intents and purposes, my life is over.'

Arabella took his hand and squeezed it. 'Poor us. Nothing to look forward to except the treadmill. Years of cold, draughty platforms and crowded, smelly commuter trains. Years of jobs we despise and colleagues we dislike – all to pay off the mortgage on a suburban matchbox that we didn't much care for the day we bought it.'

Hugo stretched out an arm and grabbed a champagne bottle. It was empty. With a sigh, he tapped it away and it rolled gently down the bank and plopped into the river. 'How about one last adventure before we ring down the curtain on our youth?' he murmured.

'One last fling,' said Celia, 'before we take our places in the galley. I swear I can almost feel the shackles around my wrists and ankles.' She nudged the man beside her. 'Patrick, you are the only one of us in line for a double first. Now is the time to prove that you can dump astrophysics for a moment or two, descend to the foothills of Mount Olympus and put your teeming intellect at the disposal of this forlorn little assembly.'

Patrick pushed his spectacles over the dome of his forehead where his sparse ginger hair was already receding. 'I have to confess,' he said, 'that I do have the germ of an idea.'

'Let's hope it's catching,' said Hugo gloomily.

Arabella threw a cushion at him. 'Relax everybody,' she said. 'Patrick has it all worked out.'

'Well,' Patrick conceded, 'as a matter of fact, I have.' He reached into his pocket and produced three slips of paper which he handed around.

Hugo put a hand to his throbbing head. 'Good lad! It's all typed out. Trying to decipher Patrick's hieroglyphics after all that booze would have tipped me over the edge.'

Celia was on her feet, her sharp, bird-like features set in a heavy frown. 'I hope this is just a joke,' she said severely.

Hugo flicked on a lighter and reread the instructions by the light of the flame. 'We cannot blame Patrick,' he groaned. 'We asked for it and we have got it.'

Arabella raised her head from the paper, her vivid blue eyes rounding with astonishment. 'But what if we refuse?'

'You will have to pay a forfeit,' replied Patrick smoothly. 'Defaulters will be provided with a mount from the Saddle Club and will have to ride the length of the High at eight o'clock in the morning dressed as Lady Godiva – or Lord Godiva, as appropriate.'

'We would be thrown in jail!' protested Celia.

'I haven't time to grow my hair!' wailed Arabella.

'It's right in the middle of the rush hour,' grumbled Hugo.

'There won't be any shirkers,' said Patrick firmly. 'I know my friends too well to worry that any of you will run up the white flag. We will meet for dinner next Saturday at the Pig & Bristle. You will make your mission reports and then we shall take a vote on who has performed best and present him or her with a suitable prize.'

'But what about you, Patrick?' complained Hugo. 'You are getting away scot-free.'

Patrick stood up and stretched. 'I am the umpire. There are many aspects of the project that I like but that appealed to me most.'

* * *

A week later, the four of them duly met for dinner at the Pig & Bristle. They took a small room on the upper floor where they would be free from interruption. By agreement, they postponed any discussion of their adventures until the plates had been cleared away and the port had done a round of the table. Patrick paid for the bottle. 'Not,' he assured his friends, 'to assuage any guilt that I might have felt for dodging the draft, but to loosen your tongues!'

Celia shuffled her notes into a semblance of order before rising to her feet. 'It was rather daunting,' she began, 'to read my instructions and discover that it was Dr Myles Medlar whom I had to ... interview ... accost would, perhaps, be a better word. He wrote some of the earliest books on how to have a successful marriage but

18

none of the bookshops that I visited stocked them. Eventually, after a feverish search, I picked up a copy of *Conjugal Concord* in a barrow in the Charing Cross Road.

'I skimmed through it on the train. It was very disjointed and seemed to me to be the work of many hands. On the back cover there was a photograph of the author standing with his wife on the deck of a liner. He was plump and balding and had a pencil moustache and gaps between his teeth.

'I had used the publisher's blurb and the telephone directory to find his address and alighted at a small suburban station near Croydon and walked the rest of the way. This took me a little time because it was a warm day and I was wearing a blue cotton dress which reached to my ankles. The garment had a starched white collar with matching cuffs. With my fringe of fair hair and pink cheeks, I flattered myself that I looked, if not attractive, then wholesome.

'The house was unremarkable: small, detached, with a pebbledash front and a neat garden bounded by a white picket fence. Stone rabbits in various poses played on the lawn and a short gravel path lined with busy Lizzies led to the porch. A net curtain twitched and I caught a glimpse of a plastic replica of Rodin's statue of *The Kiss*.

'I pressed the bell and listened to approaching footsteps. From inside, a voice like a foghorn bellowed, "Is that you, Myles?" There followed a frightful crash.

'The door opened. *"Who are you? Why are you here?"* It was Dr Medlar. Without waiting for an answer, he bent down to scoop up fragments of broken china. "I never see clients without an appointment," he grumbled. "*Never! Ever!* It is one of my rules. Well, don't dither on the doorstep. Come in if you must."

'As he led me through the sitting room, he gestured towards the piles of books on the carpet. *Harmony of Hearts ... Launch Out on Love…* Business was rather slow, he said. There were more in the garage.

'I heard something scuttling down the stairs and a corgi hurtled into the room. It made a dive for the Doctor's heels and he give a little cry and rushed me into a small study, slamming the door behind him. He was breathing heavily and flapped feebly at a moth which had flown out of the net curtains.

'"It was very remiss of you," he said, "very remiss indeed not to have telephoned for an appointment. When Doris is having one of her little turns, I try to meet clients in the park where it is quieter. What did you say your name was?"

'"Chastity. Chastity Chase."

'"What an unusual name. Very unusual indeed." He pressed a piece of sticking plaster on his forehead back into place and waved me to a small sofa covered in faded chintz. "Relax Miss Chase. It is so important to relax." He moved to a chair behind his desk and fastened the buttons of his waistcoat.

'"You will want to know something about me. I never meant to become a consultant but my hand was forced. People read my books but that was not enough. They wanted to bring their problems to me, to tap into a rich seam of knowledge and experience covering all aspects of human relationships." He reached for a pad. "I usually charge ten guineas for a preliminary appointment but under the … circumstances, I am prepared to reduce it to five. I assume that will be satisfactory?"

'I nodded.

'"Very well, Miss Chase," he leaned forward and squinted at me from under heavy eyebrows, "now tell me what I can do for you."

'I dabbed at my eyes. "I have always been a timid girl, Dr Medlar. I am shy with strangers. My father and mother were very religious and very strict. I grew up in a small, isolated community which made its own rules. Transgressions were severely punished. When we went out we were supervised by a member of our family. Girls were never allowed to meet boys on their own. Now that I am at university and expected to mix with male undergraduates, I am finding it very difficult to cope."

'The doctor made a little tent of his fingers. "I can see that we are on delicate ground but I need you to expand a little on what you have told me."

'I lowered my eyes and tortured my handkerchief into a knot. 'This is so painful for me, Dr Medlar. I have never talked to anyone the way I am talking to you. Perhaps, if you were to sit on the sofa with me, it would make it easier."

'The doctor pursed his lips. "It is a little unorthodox, Miss Chase, but not, I think, unprofessional." He rose to his feet and placed himself at the opposite end of the sofa.

'I smiled my thanks and continued. "My mother and father warned me never to kiss a young man until I was married. They said that it led to … other things."

'The doctor cleared his throat. "It can do. I won't deny it. Sometimes people let their feelings run away with them. Discipline and control can be taught. In my book–"

' *"Doctor!"* I interjected. "You *must* help me! When my girlfriends go to the cinema with their young men, they sit in the back row and look forward to the picture starting. But when the lights go down and I see what's happening all around me, I … I get so nervous … I have to run outside."

'"Leaving your young man inside. He must be very disappointed."

'I blew my nose. "He is probably pleased to be rid of a clumsy, timid girl who is too shy even to kiss him."

'"Ah. Is that the problem?" He crossed the room to a bookshelf and took down a copy of *Launch Out on Love*. "I have devoted the whole of Chapter Four to kissing. The book was published at fifteen shillings. You can have it for ten."

' *"Oh! Doctor Medlar!* You don't understand. I'm sure your books are wonderful but they deal with the theory of kissing … and other things. I need to be taught the practice of kissing … and other things … by a professional … a qualified practitioner … in the calm, clinical atmosphere of a consulting room – not in a cinema with an overexcited youth pawing me and all those people around."

' *"Miss Chase!* You *cannot* mean what I think you mean!" Dr Medlar had been trying to place as much distance between himself and his client as the small sofa allowed. Now he attempted to rise but I took his arm and placed it around my waist. "Would it help," I whispered, "if we looked at the pictures in your book?"

' *"No! It would not!"* The Doctor groaned and, reclaiming his arm, put his head in his hands. "Oh,

Chastity! Chastity! A malevolent Providence has sent you to torment me. For years I have dreamed that a sweet, innocent young girl might come knocking on my door asking for help and I would set her feet on primrose paths. But now that it has happened…"

'He was too overcome to continue and I took him in my arms, placed his head upon my lap and gently stroked his sparse hair.

'"You are a dear creature," he said at length, "and perhaps you will not think me so unmanly when you learn of some of the trials that I have undergone. I was brought up in Kent. My father was a miner and worked day shifts, so I rarely saw him. We were poor and my mother took in washing to make the money go further.

'"They must have made many sacrifices for I wanted for very little. When the lending library called, we could not afford to pay the few pennies it cost to borrow books but the nice woman lent them to me for nothing. I always had my head in a book and dreamed of growing up and fighting dragons, rescuing distressed damsels and winning my spurs in knightly combat.

'"My mother had no time for me. Nature had made her a kindly woman but the struggles of life had taken all softness from her. What affection remained, she gave to her dog, a corgi called Shep. When I came to my mother for a hug and a kiss, she would push me away and the little brute, which was insanely jealous, would savage me, nipping me in the ankles, scuttling after me going *nip, nip, nip* with its sharp little teeth until it had driven me from the room.

'"I had to leave school early to help bring some money in but I got a job in the local library and went on educating myself at evening classes. That's where I met

Doris. She loved animals and was training to become a vet but her eyesight let her down and she was never able to qualify.

"'This was a great blow to her and made her miserable. I married her because I was sorry for her. My parents had died and with what the sale of the house brought in and what I had saved we were not badly off. We went to a boarding house in Margate for a few days for our honeymoon. One afternoon, we were strolling through the town when she saw a corgi in a pet shop.

"'I begged her not to buy it and we had our first row, but Doris could be very stubborn when her mind was made up and she made me buy it and bring it home. She called it Sergeant. It hated me from the very first moment. Whenever I tried to give Doris a kiss or a cuddle, it would come snuffling round my ankles looking for a piece of bare flesh to sink its teeth into.

"'I asked Doris to get rid of it but she would not hear of it." He pulled a handkerchief from his sleeve and blew his nose. "If we had been able to have children, we might have managed but they did not come along and we started to lead separate lives.

"'I used to go up to London in the evenings and not return until the early hours of the morning. Sometimes I walked the streets until I was exhausted. Other times I visited prostitutes. As soon as they found out that I wanted nothing from them but their company, they used to relax and have a drink and talk.

"'They fascinated me. They seemed to lead a hundred different lives. The experiences that they had had astonished me. If people could learn from their successes and failures, they would be saved much heartache. That is when I started writing. In the train, on the way home, I would write down everything that I had heard and these conversations formed the basis of my books. They did not sell very well. Most of them will have to be pulped." A tear rolled down his cheek.

'Somewhere in the house a bell rang. The dog started barking and scratching at the door. The Doctor stood up and gave a deep sigh. "You must go. I will let you out of the back door. Doris will be wanting her tea."'

***

Hugo refilled his glass and half emptied it again. Thus fortified, he stood up and embarked upon his tale. 'I put my bicycle in the guard's van and arrived at Winchester station just as the troop train was pulling out on its way to Southampton. Some wag had put a notice in a window saying, *Next Stop Mombasa!* People who had been lining the streets to watch the regiment marching through the town were starting to drift away.

'I took to the lanes as soon as I was in open countryside and must have cycled the best part of ten miles in steady rain when I stopped at a large gate which barred the entrance to a wood. Nailed to it was a newly painted notice which read, *Bastion Hall, Private Property, Keep Out!*

'I stood under a large oak, opened the saddlebag and pulled out a battledress, beret and a pair of Army boots. I put these on, stuffed my jacket and flannels into the bag and lowered my bike into a deep ditch which ran beside the lane. I covered it with some branches, climbed over the gate and squelched up the sodden pathway.

'I had stopped for a moment to look at some young pheasants which were huddled together in a cage when I heard a shout. A horseman came galloping towards me on a large chestnut mount. He had grey hair cut very short, a face like a slab of undercooked beef and a bristling moustache. A black retriever scampered along behind him.

'I darted into the trees and crouched down behind the pheasant cage. *"It's no good skulking in there!"* he bawled. *"Come out where I can see you!"*

'As I emerged from my hiding place, he shouted again, "Warren! Warren! Where's my bloody gamekeeper? Never there when I want him!" He slapped his riding crop against a highly polished hunting boot.

'An answering shout came from further up the track and in a few moments the gamekeeper panted up to us. "Sorry, General. I was –"

'"Never mind that now, man. I have caught another of those blasted draft dodgers. Probably cutting across to the railway station."

'"Shall I call –"

'"*No!* Leave the Military Police out of it! I will deal with this myself. March the scoundrel up to the Hall." The General dug his spurs into the side of his horse and thundered back up the ride.

'The gamekeeper gestured at me with his shotgun and I walked ahead of him.

'He started to chuckle. "What made you come this way? You must be stark raving mad. General Bertie will probably have you shot."

'"I think I have heard of him," I said timidly.

'"If you haven't, you ruddy well should have. General Sir Bertram Brassard. *Brimstone Brassard!* That's what they call him."

'The path brought us to the back drive and a few minutes later I passed under an archway into the stable yard. A groom was rubbing down a horse in one of the loose boxes. "Follow me," growled the General as he strode into the tack room and sat at a table.

'Shiny saddles were perched on a wooden horse. Bridles hung from hooks. Chests for blankets were sited around the floor and on the wall was a glass case festooned with rosettes of different colours.

'I stood in front of him in my soaking beret and battledress and muddy boots.

' *"Hat off!"* he barked. "Come to attention! Name, rank, number and unit?"

'The answers I gave were hopelessly inadequate.

'"*Insubordination!* Absent without leave! Desertion in the face of the enemy! Sergeant Warren, take him to the guardroom!"

'"Sir!" Warren clattered to a halt behind me. "*Prisoner, about turn!* Lef', Ri', Lef', Ri', Lef', Ri', Lef'! *Right wheel!*"

'Warren marched me to the front of the house where the General pushed open the door and took the lead as we progressed through the hall. He pointed to some of the military portraits hanging from the walls. "*All Brassards!* Seven generations! General Frederick, the hero of Pondicherry. General Lionel fought at Blenheim. General Vincent commanded the Light Cavalry at Waterloo. General Douglas won a VC at Festubert."

'A woman called out from one of the large, brilliantly lit reception rooms. "Is that you, Bertie?"

'"Yes, Millie."

'"What are you doing?"

'"Attending to military business."

'"Your bath is running, Bertie. People will be arriving in twenty minutes. Please don't be late. You know how much this evening means to Clive and Sophie."

'We descended a flight of stone steps and arrived in a large vaulted cellar. Immediately on the left was a small room containing a cast-iron safe. The open side, including the door grill, consisted of thick steel bars, spaced about twelve inches apart, which ran from the floor to the ceiling.

'"In there," grunted the General. He locked me in and both men went back up the stairs.

'There was not much to look at beside the distempered walls and racks of wine bottles. At the far end, there was a grating and I heard the sound of car wheels on gravel, the chatter of voices and doors being slammed shut.

'Two children, a boy and a girl, came down the stairs. They had sticks over their shoulders and were chanting, "We are changing the guard at Buckingham Palace." They stopped as soon as they saw me. "I'm Nigel. She's Fiona," announced the boy. "Are you on guard?"

'"Something like that," I replied.

'"Then we will have to think of another game," said the girl rather resentfully.

'"Let's do drill," suggested the boy. "You know, the way Grandpa does it."

'An altercation ensued as to who would issue the commands and who would have to obey them. This was only resolved when I agreed to give the orders while Nigel and Fiona strutted up and down.

'The laughter only ended when their elder sister appeared to ask what all the noise was about. Ignoring their cries of protest, she put an end to the parade and chased the two up the stairs.

'She returned quickly, closing the door quietly behind her and padded down the steps in her stockinged feet. Coming right up to the bars, she stood facing me. She was wearing a white dress with a blue sash around her waist and a matching bow in her hair. "I'm Lavinia," she said. "I'm nearly sixteen and quite grown up."

'She grabbed hold of the bars, her china-blue eyes wide with excitement. "Is it true that you are on the run from the Army? Upstairs I heard someone say that there is a huge manhunt and all the ports and airfields have been alerted."

'"Are they saying that?" I asked her.

'"Gosh, I admire you," she whispered, pressing herself against the bars. "You seem so calm in the middle of this maelstrom. If only I could help you escape. If only we could both run away. Wouldn't it be wonderful if we were handcuffed together like the man and the woman in *The Thirty-Nine Steps*! Of course, it would be terribly embarrassing when I wanted to change into my pyjamas. I would detest you at first and say dreadfully cruel things but then we would fall in love!"

'Several people came wandering down the stairs with glasses in their hands. Lavinia took one look at them and fled. The new arrivals had already had a few drinks and probably assumed that I was on security duty.

'"Clive used to give bottle-parties here in the old days," someone said. "He put black crêpe paper on the walls and turned it into a nightclub."

'Soon the room was almost full. An exotic creature in a gold lamé blouse and slinky silk trousers swayed up to me and leaned against the bars. "I'm Melanie," she breathed in a husky voice. "I have always wanted to be an anthropologist like you … to live for years in mud huts among African tribes and hunt with bows and arrows … and then go to Cambridge and write the most brilliant thesis on the Kikuyu." She exhaled a cloud of smoke from a Balkan Sobranie cigarette. "How dare they send you to Kenya and order you to gun down all those wonderful black people!"

'Mrs Berry, a woman with a brisk, managing air had been hovering impatiently close by and Melanie, catching sight of her, retreated.

'"Jane Berry," she said, moving up to the bars and pressing my hand in hers. "I am the chairman of the constituency's selection committee. Many of my colleagues are here this evening. Colonel Corncrake is standing down at the next election and it is no secret that we were going to nominate Clive Brassard, the General's son, to replace him. Sophie, his wife, is charming and they have two delightful children. It is the second safest seat in the country."

'She turned and gestured frantically to a couple who were coming down the stairs. "*Clive! Sophie!* Please join us." She lowered her voice. "Clive, I don't know when I have been so shaken. We have all read about the bullying of recruits in the armed services and the dreadful living conditions in some of the camps. This young man, this heroic young man, has been taking on the bigots and autocrats among the brass hats single-handed. *I repeat, single-handed*! That is why he has been lured to this place and incarcerated in this dungeon, to be gawped at by all the world like an animal in a zoo."

'During this speech, Clive's stocky, well-upholstered frame had been swelling like a pressure cooker on the point of exploding. He was on the point of utterance when Mrs Berry held up an imperious hand. "No! *Please!* Let me finish. The General is a martinet of the old school and too hidebound to change his ways but there is no excuse for his son. The Party is trying to project a gentler, more caring image and, in you Clive, and your young family, we thought we had found our new torch-bearer." She shook her head sorrowfully. "It is deeply disappointing. The committee will have much to consider … and reconsider."

'Mrs Berry responded to a querulous cry from her hostess of, *"Where on earth is everybody?"* and returned up the stairs followed by the other guests.

'Clive lingered for a moment longer. "I'm frightfully sorry, old man," he muttered between gritted teeth, "but there seems to have been the most awful cock-up. What makes it worse is that I'm blessed if I know where the key has got to." Sophie gave me a brave smile and blinked away a tear. Arms tight around each other for comfort, they too mounted the stairs.

'Some of the guests stayed for dinner and everyone forgot about me. It was close to midnight when Lady Brassard paid me a visit. She was wearing a lavender-blue dressing gown and bedroom slippers and carried herself as upright as if she was balancing a coronet on her head.

'"I don't know who you are," she said, "or what you are doing in this house. I have heard so many theories it has made me feel quite dizzy." She produced a large key from her pocket and, holding it with both hands, unlocked the door of my prison and released me. "I had to wait until Bertie was asleep. The key was under his pillow." From another pocket, she pulled a brown paper bag.

'"You are a foolish young man," she said, holding my eyes, "who has caused the family much embarrassment, but I do not think that you are wholly wicked. In the bag you will find some roast duck left over from dinner." She handed me an envelope. "The contents of this are yours if you promise me, on your honour, to keep quiet about this little adventure."

'Without waiting for me to speak, she gathered up her gown, hurried up the steps and led the way to the back door. "Go back the way you came," were her last words to me. This I did.'

***

Arabella had drunk three glasses of port and was rather flushed in the face. 'I'm not quite sure that I can stand up like the other two,' she giggled, 'so I hope you won't mind if I tell my story sitting down.

'I used my own name throughout and just prayed that I would not get into too much trouble. I knew the town quite well because I had been to stay there with friends from school. The house that I was making for was an Elizabethan mansion that was close to the Law Courts and had been used by circuit judges for many years.

'I parked my car in a small road and followed a narrow path that ran between two properties before emerging into the main road. The path separated the gardens of the two houses and was bounded on both sides by a wooden fence.

'It was dusk and getting cold and my only cover was a horse blanket. My eyes were fixed on the back of the house to my right, which was my destination, and I was startled to hear a voice from the garden to my left call out, "Who is there?"

'"It's only Arabella," I replied.

'"And who is Arabella?" came the answer.

'"I'm on my way to see Judge Garrett," I said.

'"It did not occur to you to use the front door, I suppose."

'"I parked my car at the back. It seemed to be the quickest way."

'The speaker shone a torch at the top of the fence and I stood on tiptoe and presented my face for inspection. It appeared that I had passed the test because the man turned away and the torch flickered over a large wire-mesh pen. Inside was a large snake. "That's an African python," I said. "Not full grown at a guess."

'"Right both times," the man replied. "Sybil is having her supper and she doesn't like being disturbed." I started to apologise but he cut me short. "Anyway, where did you learn about snakes?"

'"In Uganda. My father was a game warden."

'"Most people are terrified of snakes but you and I know that they make very affectionate pets if they are handled carefully."

'"Yes." It was on the tip of my tongue to add that it saddened me to see them out of their natural habitat and kept in a cage.

'"Well, next time you are passing, ring the bell and I will introduce you." He bade me goodnight and went inside his house.

'The sky had darkened swiftly and a few drops of rain were starting to fall. I pushed through a side gate and jogged on the steps for a few moments before tapping on the pane of the back door. A light came on and a window was pushed open.

'A woman's face emerged and then disappeared again. The door opened and the woman looked me up and down. *"Good gracious, girl!* What are you doing standing there with no clothes on?"

'"I'm afraid I have had a bit of an accident," I said breathlessly.

'"Come in. Come in at once … but keep your voice down. The Judge is still at dinner."

'*"The Judge!"* I exclaimed.

'She gave me a sharp look. "Mr Justice Garrett. You haven't done anything wrong, I hope. If you have, you have come to the wrong place."

' *"Beryl!"* There came an imperious summons from beyond the doorway. "What *is* going on? Who are you talking to at this time of night?"

'The housekeeper rolled her eyes and hurried out of the scullery. I just had time to check that the hasp on the sash window had not been fastened before she came bustling back.

'"The Judge is asking for you." She took my arm.

' *"Do I go like this!"* I pointed to my unkempt hair, the primitive blanket that covered me and my naked feet.

'"Like that," she said firmly. "When the Judge says '*Straight away*!' that's what he means."

'She led me down a narrow, dimly lit passage to the dining room. The Judge was wearing a velvet smoking jacket and was sitting at the end of a long refectory table. The only light came from four tall candles and the fire in the big hearth. Around the walls were portraits of legal luminaries from the distant past.

'The Judge pushed back his chair and stood up. "I am Mervyn Garrett," he growled. "What is your name?"

'"Arabella, Sir."

'"Arabella who?"

'"Just Arabella for the moment, Sir."

'"*Oh! So it's like that!* Are you wanted by the police?"

'"They may be looking for me," I replied.

'The Judge waved Beryl from the room with an injunction to return quickly with something for me to put on. "And bring a comb with you," he called after her.

'"You are shivering. Stand closer to the fire." He reached for the decanter and poured out a glass of port. While I was drinking it, he was shooting glances at me from under heavy white eyebrows. Then he pointed to the sideboard. "You will find some remains of a roast chicken. Eat it up. We can talk later."

'Beryl returned with a scarlet robe trimmed in ermine, a pair of corduroy slippers and a comb. The

Judge turned the robe over in his hands. "Is that all you could find? What about your own clothes?"

'"The girl is much taller than I am, Sir. She would look ridiculous."

'"She could hardly look more absurd than she does at the moment." He threw the robe over a chair. "Very well. Let her wear it." He waited until I had finished my meal. Beryl cleared away the dishes and they both went out of the room and left me to change.

'The port made me feel light-headed. I cast off the blanket and stood in front of the fire and combed my long fair hair into a semblance of order. In the large gilt-framed mirror over the mantelpiece, I saw the door nudge open. I have acute hearing and I heard a sigh. I felt sure that the Judge was watching me and some spirit of devilment made me linger there.

'Then I dressed and walked slowly around the room looking at the pictures and letting them look at me. The scarlet robe, the firelight on my hair – I don't think that they would have been disappointed.

'"You seem to have made yourself at home," said the Judge as he pushed the door open. "Suppose you stop behaving as if you were taking part in a fashion show and give an account of yourself." He pointed to a chair and took one next to it.

'I told him that I had been to the County Show that day. "I was with Rupert, a friend from university. He is a rather bookish type and I was curious to see how he would behave at an agricultural fair. Rupert's idea of giving a girl a good time is to walk up and down his room spouting love sonnets from Keats when he could be holding the real thing in his arms and kissing her."

'The Judge canted his head to one side and pursed his lips and I felt my cheeks burning. "I do hope," I added, "that I am not giving the impression that I am fast because I am not. But I am a romantic and it does seem to me a terrible waste for a good-looking boy to spend so much time with his head in those musty old books when he could be having fun."

'"When I was your friend's age, I spent quite a lot of time with my head in musty old books," observed the Judge. "Go on."

'"Rupert drove me to the fair and I took him around the sheds and we looked at cattle and pigs and chickens, and then went and sat beside the main ring where the heavy horse parade was just finishing. I love watching the Suffolk punches with their plaited manes and hooves the size of soup plates but poor Rupert found the whole thing dreadfully tedious.

'"He pulled out a pocket edition of Byron's poems and started to read them and I went off to the beer tent, drank too much and got rather tight. When I came back, we quarrelled. I told him that I was sorry that I had brought him to the fair and that he was one of the dullest, most predictable, most boring characters that I had ever had the misfortune to meet.

'"He was hurt and angry. 'What do you expect me to do?' he snapped. 'Stand on my head?'

'"Well, it might liven things up a bit," I told him.

'"But he just sulked. He wasn't that sort of person, he said. Then he turned on me. 'Why don't you do something amazing, Arabella? *Or are you all talk and no action?*'

'"You will soon know," I cried. *"Just watch me!"* There was an empty horsebox behind us and I ran inside it and threw off every stitch of clothing. Then I raced down the ramp like a whippet after a hare. I vaulted the rope and streaked across the ring.

'"There were hundreds of people around the ring and more in the stands. For a second there was a sort of stunned silence and then whoops and cheers came from all sides. One of the stewards raised his bowler to me as I passed. Someone blew '*Gone away!*' on a hunting horn and a terrier broke loose and chased after me, barking its head off.

'"Two policemen grabbed me when I reached the far side and tried to cover me up with their helmets. They agreed where to put one of them but came close to blows deciding where to place the other and the crowd loved it. The coppers found a horse blanket from somewhere and chucked it over me and then bundled me into a squad car. I sat between them as we drove to the police station.

'"When we got there, one of them went to fetch a WPC. I asked the other one to wind up the window and while he was doing that I nipped out of the other door and into a maze of little streets. I had a good start on them and they never stood a chance of catching me."

'The Judge cut off the end of a cigar and lit up. "What puzzles me is why did you come here of all places?"

'"It was getting dark," I told him, "and cold and starting to rain. I had to find somewhere warm and dry before nightfall."

'The Judge refilled my glass. "You have behaved very foolishly. You realise that, don't you?"

'I lowered my head. "I am in your hands, Sir."

'"You are." He drew on his cigar until the tip glowed. "And I'm not at all happy about harbouring a fugitive from justice."

'"The police don't know my name."

'"They will soon find out," he grunted. "Your photograph will be all over the local paper. And what about your friend? Won't he be worried about you?"

'"Rupert's one idea will be to put as many miles between him and me as possible," I replied.

'The Judge reached under the table and pressed a bell. "You had better spend the night here. Beryl will show you to your bedroom. I will decide what to do with you in the morning."

'"I'm sorry to have caused so much trouble," I said. "I have never done anything like this before. Please don't be too hard on me."

'"We will see." He gave me a rather strange look, handed me over to Beryl and wished me a good night.

'Beryl led me up a wide staircase to a gallery and showed me my bedroom. The bed was rather small for such a large room. The walls were panelled in dark oak and a china jug and ewer stood on a table. She opened a door to reveal a tiny bathroom and then went to the windows and drew the curtains close together.

'"Please sit down," she said. "I want to talk to you." I sat on the bed.

'"I am sure you are a nice, well-brought-up girl," she began, "but I'm sorry that you came here and I wish that you were not spending the night."

'"I'm sorry too–"

'She held up her hand. "Please let me go on. You ought to know that the Judge is not really a family man. He and his wife have been separated for years and they now live apart. He has a daughter but he never sees her. He is in his mid-fifties but he seems to have the energy of a man half his age." She took off her glasses and polished them on the sleeve of her dress.

'"Beryl, what is it–"

'"What I am trying to say is that he has a forceful personality and there have been problems with some of his relationships. There has been a certain amount of gossip … much of it malicious. He is taking early retirement."

'"Where is the Judge's bedroom?"'

'Beryl raised her eyebrows but I sensed that she welcomed the question. "Next to this one."

'I waited for her to say something more but she remained silent. "Beryl, I am as much in the dark as ever."

'She shook her head. "I have probably said too much already. We all have our little quirks. I am very fond of the Judge and, after all, I work for him. So … goodnight, my dear … and sleep well." She went to the door, removed the key and locked my door on the outside. I was a prisoner.

'I took off the robe and had a bath. There was a nightie under my pillow – probably one of Beryl's because it was too small – but I put it on. Then I turned off the bedside light and knelt down to say my prayers. I could hear the Judge next door humming snatches from Gilbert and Sullivan and found it difficult to compose my thoughts.

'The floor consisted of bare boards which were partly covered by rugs so I was surprised when my knees encountered a depression in an otherwise smooth surface. I turned on the light again, raised the valance and peered under the bed.

'The four castors rested on a rectangle of linoleum. On the two long sides, a shallow groove, like a miniature railway line, ran between them. The bed could not be moved into the room or pushed sideways because the head was fixed to the wall.

'I ran my fingers up and down the panelling searching for the places where it "gave". Very soon, I was able to trace the shape of a door, half the normal height but wide enough to enable the bed to slide through the wall into the adjoining bedroom. The lines scored in the linoleum were proof that this was no fantasy.

'I sat on the bed and cursed my folly. I had told a pack of lies and deliberately placed myself in the hands of a notorious philanderer. If things turned out badly, people would say that I had asked for trouble and got it.

'I went to the window. There was a flowerbed beneath me but I was much too high to risk jumping. Several feet to my left there was a downpipe. It looked fairly sturdy. If I could reach it, I should be able to get to the ground.

'I breathed a short prayer and then climbed out onto the sill. There was a horrid grating sound as I forced the window back so that I could get around it and then I had to let my legs swing free and support myself by my arms as I moved along the sill. I started to panic and scrabbled with my toes against the brickwork and managed to rest a foot on the slender branch of a climbing plant.

'There was a heart-stopping moment as I lunged with my right hand, grabbed the pipe and hauled myself across the gap. Level with my eyes was a chink of light which came from one of the windows of the Judge's bedroom. I pulled myself up a little and peered through a gap in the curtains into the room.

'The Judge was sitting on a chair beside his bed facing the wall and stealthily working a bolt backwards and forwards. As I watched, he stopped and listened. Then he started again. My first instinct had been to slide down the pipe as fast as I could and make a run for it. Fury gave me the strength to lower myself slowly and silently and as I descended, a crazy idea took shape in my head.

'In the sky, broken cloud and a half moon gave me the light I needed. I trotted along the edge of the lawn, through the first side gate and then the second that let me into the garden of the neighbouring house.

'Sybil was coiled up on the floor of a wooden hut inside her enclosure. She raised her head as I opened the door and a spasm of fear ran through me as I saw her eyes glittering. But she was drowsy after her supper and did not mind being picked up.

'I was worried about the scullery window but it had not been locked and Sybil unwound herself from my neck and waist, slithered through the opening and stretched out along the sink and draining board. I followed her and put her over my shoulders when we went up the stairs. I was in luck again. My door was locked but the key was still on the outside.

'There was enough light from the gallery for what I needed to do. I tucked Sybil into my bed with her pretty head on the pillow. Then I placed my ear against the panelling. I heard a faint sound from the other side. It was time to flee.

'Back in my car, I re-dressed and sat in darkness with the window down. When I heard a scream and saw the lights on the top floor come on, I drove off. The next day, I returned Beryl's nightie by first-class post with a note of thanks.'

***

After a vote was taken, Arabella was declared the winner. Celia and Hugo had tied for second place.

'It would have been nice to have beaten Hugo,' said Celia.

'Well, you didn't actually manage to kiss Dr Medlar,' said Patrick. 'I'm afraid that probably cost you a few marks.'

Hugo opened the envelope that he had taken away from Bastion Hall and announced that Lady Brassard was paying for their dinner.

A few days later, Arabella had to warn Patrick that he should regard their friendship as at an end unless he refrained from calling her 'Anaconda'.

Fetch !

'Oh! Mother!'

'What *is* it, Sarah?'

'I wanted to have a good cry all by myself and that stupid dog of yours came in and spoiled everything!'

'Fetch only wants to help. He's really very bright, like all Welsh sheepdogs. Anyway, why were you crying?'

'I have been looking in the mirror. Why am I so plain, Mother? You and Daddy look OK.'

'You are very pleasant looking, darling.'

'That's just a kind way of saying the same thing. I have a face like a horse. Long and thin.'

'*Nonsense!* You have very nice hair and an excellent figure.'

Sarah sighed. 'And it's so dull here. I'm nearly thirty and I never seem to meet any nice men. In fact, I don't meet any young men. Period.'

'Well, darling, you can't say that we haven't tried. I entered you for the tennis competition. The mixed doubles, wasn't it?'

'My partner was the most dreadful bore. It was a relief to get knocked out in the first round.'

'And there was that cocktail party at the Golf Club.'

'Most of the men were married or twice my age. There was only one good-looking chap. We talked for a few minutes but I could tell that he was longing to escape. Are you happy, Mother? Does Dad make you happy?'

'Of course he does.'

'Why "of course"? He's only interested in his golf. And you have your coffee mornings and your bridge parties.'

'And the dogs. Smudge has a litter every year. I train up some of the puppies and find them good homes and sell the others. It pays your father's wine bill.'

'The training doesn't amount to much. I saw Patch yesterday running along the High Street on some futile errand.'

'Patch ought to be given a medal. He goes to the newsagent first thing in the morning and brings back the *Daily Mirror*. Mrs Lakin has terrible rheumatism. She told me that she wouldn't know what to do without Patch.'

'Golf and bridge and dogs doing errands. You must admit, Mother, it is not very exciting.'

'There are different sorts of happiness, Sarah. At our age, your father and I don't want excitement. We are fortunate to have reasonable health and still be in our right minds. We both have a small pension and can afford to return hospitality. Whatever is left over goes on giving you an allowance so that you can have a bit of fun.'

'But I *don't* have fun, Mother.'

'Perhaps you should change your job. Working as a secretary for a firm of solicitors in a seaside town isn't very inspiring.'

'But it pays quite well and I can live at home.'

'Maybe you should move to London, but then we would miss you dreadfully.'

Sarah kissed her mother. 'I can't bear London. I love the country around here – the marshland and the rushes, the gulls wheeling and screaming, the huge skies and the sea.'

'And you do have your own space. Whenever you feel stifled by living with your aged parents, you can always go to the beach house.'

'I love that little house with its white clapboards and the rickety veranda. I sometimes slip out after dinner and walk down the lane and spend the night there.'

'I know you do.'

'But you don't mind?'

'Of course not. It's very isolated but I'm sure it is perfectly safe. And you are a good swimmer. I never worry about you.'

Sarah laughed. 'I don't mind you spying on me.'

'I don't call it spying. I'm watching out for you. We don't go racing any more so I keep the field glasses in my bedroom.'

'Well, you would have to be up very early to see me swimming. It's still dark when I get up. I scramble into my swimsuit–'

'Why bother with that?'

'Force of habit, I suppose.'

'You should start breaking a few habits. It might do you good.'

'Anyway, I run across the beach and try to time it so that I reach the water just as the sun is coming up. On a fine day, it's … it's magical … that's what it is.'

'And then you have your swim. But as soon as you heard that motorbike coming up the lane, you scampered back to the safety of your lair.'

Sarah stared at her mother open-mouthed. 'So you know about the motorbike?'

It was her mother's turn to laugh. 'Of course I know about it. Part of the Special Boat Service or Squadron, or some such name, are in a tented camp on the downs. Don't you read the local paper?'

'That dreary rag? *Certainly not!*'

'You don't know what you are missing. The latest bulletin on the horticultural show or the knobbly-knees contest or–'

'Go on about the motorbike.'

'Well, a dozen or so commandos are just back from the Middle East. They are here for a fortnight's training. They get up in the middle of the night and take the track to the top of Gallows Head. Then they abseil down the cliff, inflate their rubber dinghy and paddle along the coast until they get to the breakwater.'

'*About fifty yards from the beach house*!'

'Yes. Where they are met by their leader. I don't know what his job is – perhaps he times them – but he looked very bored hanging around on the beach for half an hour. Anyway, I heard him yesterday putt-putting quietly along the lane. I was so intrigued that I had to get out of bed and take a look.'

'Did you see–?'

Sarah's mother affected not to have heard. Yes, she had seen him strip off and leave his shorts and sweater and a towel on the beach and run out to the line of breakers. He ran with long, loping strides. His hair was almost white from the desert sun and he was as brown as an otter.

She had swung the glasses back to that little pile of clothes on the sand. She had almost laughed out loud. It would be very naughty but it really was irresistible. If Fetch had been there, at a nod from his mistress, he would have dashed across the sand, picked them up and brought them back with him.

Sailor Boy wouldn't risk the derision of his comrades when they pulled up on the beach and found him in a state of nature. No, he would hare up to the beach house, knock on the door and ask for the return of his garments.

'Sarah, why don't you take Fetch with you tonight? He can sit on the veranda when you have your swim tomorrow morning. He loves running errands. I can think of one or two which would keep him happily occupied – and you.'

Sarah flung her arms around her mother. 'Mother, darling, *you are wicked!* Do you mean what I think you mean?'

Her mother nodded. 'A whole fortnight, Sarah! He really is very nice looking. You can offer him a cup of coffee and I don't think you need overdress.'

'*Shock and awe!*' cried Sarah. 'Things *are* looking up! *Fetch!*' She went to the kitchen to find a large piece of shortbread to present to her new accomplice.

War Games

It was close to Midsummer Day but the two men had started early and, in an open Jeep, it was a cold drive from the plains of Wiltshire to the London flat. The vehicle drew up in the courtyard of the large block. The driver got out and would have carried the general's bag to the front door but there was no need.

'I will take that,' said Dick Trench. 'You had better get back to barracks and have some breakfast.'

His driver saluted and drove away. The journey, he reflected, had been passed in almost complete silence. Major General Richard Trench did not encourage idle chatter but he was usually a little more talkative. Mind you, he had a staff job at the Ministry of Defence and there were rumours that his name was in the hat for a top job at NATO. It was hardly surprising that he had much to think about.

Dick Trench did not take the lift to the fifth floor. It was not yet seven o'clock and he told himself that Laura would be asleep and he did not want to wake her. But it would not have been the truth. He wanted to be alone. He took a seat on the sofa in the deserted hallway. He wanted to think about the conversation that he had overheard the previous evening.

An important divisional exercise over a period of three days on Salisbury Plain had just finished. He had been in command of the Red Forces, the attackers. They should have won but they had been defeated by the Blues, the defenders.

Trench had walked over to the judges' tent to say goodnight when he heard his name mentioned. It was dark outside but through the flap, by the light of a hurricane lamp, he could make out the figures of the two brigadiers. They were seated and smoking and having a drink together.

In the ordinary way, he would have alerted them to his presence and walked in, but he did not. He was feeling vulnerable, like a package that had been dropped in transit. If he was going to be unwrapped, he wanted to be by himself when he was inspected for damage.

He stepped into the shadows at the side of the tent. A large truck was parked a few feet away and there was no danger of being seen. He would be hard on himself for it afterwards but he had been greatly disturbed by the events of that day.

'Dick Trench is very sound,' one of the officers was saying, 'but this was an operation that called for dash. Verve. *Drive!*'

'The first attack went well,' commented his companion.

'Agreed,' replied the first speaker, 'but after that all momentum was lost. The Blues were let off the hook. They were given the chance to re-deploy and, from then on, the Reds never really worried them.'

'The Reds lost so much time at the road junctions. It wasn't the fault of the Military Police. They did their best to keep the columns moving.'

'Trench was responsible for most of the hold-ups. I saw one of his Intelligence Officers staring up at a signpost and then down at his map and calling an MP over for questioning. Multiply that a dozen times and it would have cost them time they could ill afford. I had a word with the IO. He said that his orders were to check the identity of the MPs and the directions that they were giving.'

'It's no wonder that the roads were choked. There were armoured cars and ten-tonners nose to tail. In a real war, they would have been strafed to hell and back. *It would have been carnage!*'

'You were involved in the planning of the exercise. Did you ever consider having some of the Blues disguised as Military Police?'

'No. It would have been too disruptive.'

'War is disruptive.'

'True, but our lords and masters wished to test a whole range of skills in command. They cannot do that if everything on wheels comes to a halt.'

'Trench was lucky that the Blues stayed behind their defences. The Reds' advance was more like a slowly moving car park. If the Firecracker had been leading the Blues, he would not have passed up an opportunity like that.'

'Firecracker Furniss! *What a thruster the man is!* He would have gone over to the attack. *It would have been a rout!*'

'Do you think that Trench has still got what it takes? He and Furniss are the only real contenders for the NATO job. It's a big step up. Promotion to lieutenant general. Probably a knighthood.'

'If you had asked me that yesterday, I would have said that there was nothing to choose between them. They both have first-rate records. Operational service in Kuwait and Iraq and then the Falklands. Furniss has a DSO; Trench an MC. But after what happened here … I would say that Furniss is way out in front.'

'Trench lost his wife. Cancer. That must have been a bad blow.'

'You are not thinking of entering a plea on those grounds? I'm afraid we can't put that sort of thing in the report.'

'I realise that, of course, but it was rotten luck.'

'One child, isn't there?'

'Just the daughter. She married a Danish farmer and settled over there.'

'You know that he remarried a couple of months ago?'

'Yes. To an American girl, I believe. How old is she?'

'Laura is still in her upper thirties. There must be twelve or more years between them. He was on a course at one of the American staff colleges. That's how they met.'

'From what I hear, she used to be a bit of a handful.'

'Now then! Remember the three taboos!'

'*Women, money and religion*!' They laughed. 'But, after all, this is not the officers' mess and I wasn't going to say anything derogatory about the girl.'

'Go on then, if you must.'

'She could have gone into films. She's certainly pretty enough.'

'How do you know?'

'I met her at a reception and we talked for a few minutes.'

'So, she gave up the chance of fame and fortune to marry a soldier!'

'Her parents are old-fashioned Bostonians. Hollywood was not part of their plans for her. They wanted her to settle down and start a family. She went to New York and worked in a fashion house. In her spare time she did a bit of acting. Amateur theatricals, that sort of thing.'

'And now?'

'Trench rents a flat in Westminster, a ten-minute walk from the MOD. She works in Covent Garden. I believe she writes a column for a fashion magazine.'

One of them yawned and stretched. Trench could see the movement silhouetted against the side of the tent.

'Do you feel like another drink?'

'No, thanks. It's been a long day. We had better turn in.'

***

Dick Trench took the lift. He opened the door to the flat very quietly but Laura was already awake. She bounded out of bed, threw her arms around him and gave him a kiss.

'You smell wonderful,' he murmured.

'*You don't!*' she giggled, pushing him gently from her. 'Kindly put your battledress–'

'Combat fatigues!'

'Whatever – in the laundry basket – and have a shower. Then come and tell me how it all went. I will put the coffee on.'

'*It was a disaster!*' He couldn't hold it back. He despised himself for it. Running straight off to mummy to have the scratch looked at, to have his eyes wiped and his nose blown. But he was bitterly disappointed in himself.

'What happened?' She stood there, facing him, her lips slightly parted, rather white about the nostrils.

'Furniss shafted me.'

'Is the NATO job off?'

'It was never on. Not for certain. Furniss is a hard man to beat.'

'*Don't do yourself down!* You volunteered for the Paras at the same time as he did. You both served in the Special Forces. You are every bit as good a man as he is.'

'On paper, maybe. But, on the ground, that counts for very little.'

'I'm talking about operational service. His record is no better than yours.'

'That was yesterday. We are talking about today.' He shook his head. 'I set my heart on that NATO job. I would have liked to have given you that – and what went with it.' He wasn't asking for pity. He simply wanted to step off cloud nine where he had been hovering for a month and hit the ground, hard – and find her still there beside him when he picked himself up.

'We could have done with the money.'

He didn't dare look at her. Perhaps the extended honeymoon was over. Maybe he was about to find out that Laura, *au fond*, was just another of those flint-hard females from the New World whose overriding concern was to find a man with pockets deep enough to pay the dressmaker's bills.

But she was teasing. Not by the smallest intonation had her voice given her away but her eyes were dancing and they did the talking for her. She took him in her arms again. 'What about the extra money?' she whispered. 'We are going to need that.'

He held her tight against him. He felt ashamed that he could have doubted her. 'Do you know something that I don't?' The words were whispered rather than spoken.

She shook her head. 'It was a prophecy, not a promise.'

He kissed her. 'I love you Laura. Sometimes it scares me how much I love you.'

She pushed him away. 'Well, go and scare yourself in the shower. Then come back and tell me about Major General Fallon Furniss. *The Firecracker isn't going to crack us!'*

Over several cups of strong black coffee, he told her. 'First, a history lesson Laura. After D-

Day, once the Allies had got into Belgium and Holland, the Germans had an unpleasant habit of infiltrating our forces with agents. Many had well-honed English or American accents and were so fluent that they could gossip about their favourite soccer or baseball team.

'They were in the uniform of the Military Police and stationed themselves at important road intersections. They turned the signposts around. They misdirected columns of infantry, tanks, supplies of ammunition and food. In short, they caused havoc.'

'Dick! You said that–'

'I'm coming to that. The day before I left for that exercise, Furniss called me in my office in the Ministry of Defence. He refused to say what it was about on the telephone. He insisted that we meet for a coffee. We went to one of those underground dives off Trafalgar Square.'

'Did he give you any hint of what it was about?'

'He said that he wanted to do me a good turn.'

'And you believed him?'

'I had no reason not to.'

'You had plenty – but let that pass.'

'We sat down. Had he warned me that he was going to talk about the divisional exercise, I would have got up and left. But he was too clever for that. He came straight out with it. He said that I would be in command of the Red Forces and that they were going to be infiltrated by bogus Military Policemen. The MPs were the key to dealing efficiently with large-scale movements of armour, infantry and supplies advancing on a wide front. The judges, he said, would be watching me very closely to see how I dealt with the problem.'

'What an SOB!' exclaimed Laura.

'I told Furniss that I would rather he had kept this information to himself. But, simpleton that I am, I believed that the information was given in good faith.'

'You could hardly disregard it.'

'I wish I had. As it was, what should have been a rapid advance was reduced to a crawl while I had the MPs screened and interrogated and the signposts checked against our maps.'

'Are you going to tackle Furniss about it?'

'What is the point? He would simply say that the tip-off came from the top and he believed it to be true.'

'What about the judges?'

'I can hardly complain to them.'

Laura went over to the mantelpiece and took down a photograph. 'You and Furniss are both in this photo?'

Trench nodded. 'We instructed at Staff College the same year.'

She studied the man's features. The long, narrow head, the deep-set eyes, the upper lip curled in what was closer to a sneer than a smile. 'He looks clever. And ruthless. And unscrupulous.'

'Maybe those are qualities that you need to get to the top. In his place, I would probably have done the same.'

'*Don't you dare say that, Dick Trench!* You know it isn't true!'

He smiled. 'I have a beautiful wife. I want to take her to Belgium. I want to have dinner with her in the Grande Place in Brussels. I want to show her off to the military top brass. I want all the wives to turn emerald green with envy. Is it so surprising that it has begun to affect my judgement?'

'*And don't make jokes like that!*' She tossed her glossy black hair around her head to cool her cheeks. 'I don't want to share my life with a man who is prepared to lie and cheat and do others down to get what he wants.'

He looked at his watch. He didn't feel like eating. He would skip breakfast and get along to the MOD. Furniss was probably driving back from the exercise playing triumphal marches from Souza. 'Furniss has got his regimental dinner tonight.'

'At the Services Club?'

'Yes. He must think that the NATO job is in the bag. He will be celebrating. We ought to go out for a meal and drown our sorrows.'

Laura put a hand on his arm, 'Oh! Darling! *I am sorry!* You must have forgotten. I have got a hen party this evening. It was arranged ages ago, before the exercise was planned.'

Trench clapped a hand to his forehead. '*Of course!* How silly of me! The excitements of the last twenty-four hours had driven it right out of my ahead. Who are the other girls? Do I know any of them?'

'I don't think so. There are no army wives. Most of them are married to businessmen.'

'Americans?'

'One or two.'

'In the fashion business?'

'Some of them.'

'Will you be back very late?'

'Well, we don't see each other very often.'

'Then, go and enjoy yourselves. Make a night of it.'

'That is sweet of you. I feel terribly guilty about abandoning you.'

He gave her a wry smile. 'Don't worry about me. I will knock some eggs together and then curl up with a bottle of scotch.'

***

Laura waited at the window to see whether Dick would turn and wave when he reached the courtyard. He did. She liked the way that he had kept his hair. He didn't look much over forty. She liked his blue eyes, the square jaw and the frank, open face. He gave her that smile again and she saluted. He was stricken but he wasn't going to show it. It touched her to the quick.

She couldn't face going in to the office. This was the day that she hoped to be giving in her notice. She telephoned the editor. 'Good morning, Krystelle. I'm halfway through that article. Would you mind terribly–'

'If you finished it at home? I'll let you off this time. Will we see you tomorrow?'

'Of course. You're an angel.'

She had no sooner replaced the receiver than it rang. It was Miriam Furniss.

'Laura, I do hope you don't mind my calling.' There was a pause. 'Are you still there, Laura?'

'Yes. Yes, I'm still here.'

'You may remember that we met at that rather grand garden party in the spring.'

'I do remember.'

'Well, I just wanted to say that Fallon feels rather awful about some advice that he gave Dick just before that exercise. Of course, he cannot say where it came from but he swears that it was from close to the very top. He is most upset.'

'It would have been nice if he could have telephoned my husband and told Dick just how upset he was.'

'You are quite right. I'm sure that he will do so. It is just that he is having a very busy day and he asked me to call you.'

'Protecting his flank, I suppose. I can't fault his tactics.'

'What was that? I don't quite follow–'

'It's not important. I hear that he is going to his regimental dinner tonight.'

'Yes. It is an important evening as well as a very enjoyable one. We have just learned that the CGS –'

'The Chief of the General Staff?'

'I keep forgetting that you are new to the ranks of the soldiers' wives. Yes, the professional head of the British Army. The great man has, apparently, altered his plans at short notice and is flying back from Brussels to come to the dinner.'

'That must be very gratifying.'

'It is a straw in the wind.'

'More than that, surely?'

'Let me just say that Fallon and I are encouraged by it.' Miriam Furniss's voice had acquired a sharper edge. 'The CGS and my husband will be sitting next to each other at the top table. An announcement will not be made until the end of the week but I shall be very surprised if Fallon does not receive some indication during the course of the evening that the outcome will be the one that we are hoping for.'

'I am delighted for you both.'

'It is far too soon to celebrate. I am only sorry that when there are winners, inevitably there must be losers.'

'My sentiments, exactly.' On that rather cool note, the conversation ended.

Laura could not remember when she had felt so angry, so hurt and upset. Until that moment she had not realised how deep the cut had gone. Did she mind for herself? It would be dishonest to deny it. But she minded a hundred times more for the man that she had married.

Her parents had been lukewarm about the marriage but she had turned down so many proposals that they were probably relieved to see her with a ring on her finger. What did she see in Dick Trench that she had not discerned in the others? She was still working on that. It might take her the rest of her days to slot all the pieces into that puzzle but, if it did, that was part of the answer.

But Dick was not yet sure of her. She could sense it. This appointment was important to him. They had only just started building a life together. The foundation stones were barely in place. Soon they would start on the walls and the roof. A setback at this stage was the last thing that he wanted. One or two successes early on would make a lot of difference. Success was like mortar. It held the bricks together.

She could not settle to her work. She reached for her address book. She wanted to talk to her friends.

***

The main reception room at the Services Club filled up quickly. Everyone was in dinner jackets. Some of the officers were wearing miniature medals. The Regiment was just back from the Middle East so there was a big turnout. Portraits of high-ranking soldiers from yesteryear hung on the walls and a pair of glittering chandeliers hung from the ceiling. It was an idyllic summer's evening. The curtains were not yet drawn and, across the road, the tops of the trees in the park were losing their golden leaves as the sun slipped behind the rooftops.

'I can't tell you lads anything – yet,' Furniss was saying. He put a finger to his lips and rolled his eyes in the direction of the CGS who, like him, was surrounded by the usual bevy of sycophants and career strategists. Inside, he was bubbling with high spirits.

'Nevertheless,' he added with a heavy wink, 'it is by no means too early to have a large glass of champagne.'

At half-past eleven, Furniss and the CGS descended the steps of the club together followed by a throng of fellow diners. They were replete with roast meat and Burgundies white and red, chased down by a very pleasant Sauternes.

As they reached the pavement, the two men turned to each other. The CGS thrust out his hand. 'I much look forward–' he began, but he never finished the sentence for, at that moment, a large silver, open-top roadster came speeding down the hill from the direction of Hyde Park Corner.

It slid to a halt in front of them, its arrival heralded by a fanfare on an old klaxon horn. There appeared to be six occupants. All were wearing cat masks from which protruded long whiskers in startling shades of orange, mauve and green. One, attired in little more than a pair of bunny ears and a fur-trimmed bikini, was producing ear-splitting sounds on a toy bugle. Two others, sporting identical hot-pink organza tutus, were having a fencing match with their sparklers. A placard in front of the windscreen, sign-written in lurid lettering, read: *In Town Tonight – Firecracker's Fillies!* The girls started to chant:

> 'Skinny dip, skinny dip,
> We are going for a skinny dip!'

'Do you *know* any of these women, Furniss?' exclaimed the CGS.

'None of them, General! On my honour, I have never set eyes on any of them before!'

'*Never set eyes on us!*' the girls wailed. '*We must be wearing too many clothes!*' To bellows of encouragement from the onlookers crowded together on the pavement and rapidly growing in number, the girls made to discard their vestigial garments.

Furniss stepped forward to the car. '*Stop this charade at once*,' he shouted, '*or I will call the police!*'

This sally was met with an explosion of party poppers which fired long, spaghetti-like streamers that stuck in his hair and ran down his jacket. Beside himself with fury and growling like a tiger at bay, he leaned over the side of the car and lunged at the occupants.

The girls pulled blowpipes from the waistbands of their garments and a fusillade of expertly directed confetti caught him full in the face. Temporarily blinded, he felt several pairs of arms seize him and he toppled headlong into the car.

As the roadster sped off, the rapt audience were treated to the sight of Furniss's lower limbs, naked but for a pair of sock suspenders, sticking straight up in the air and semaphoring a frantic protest. From the street corner, there came the flash of camera.

'If a reporter saw that,' muttered the CGS, 'we are sunk.'

A reporter did. The next morning, under the brazen headline *Suspended!* one of the less inhibited tabloids devoted the whole of the front page to the image.

∗∗∗

A week later, Laura took a call from Miriam Furniss.

'I underrated you, my dear,' she began.

'I don't know what you are talking about,' replied Laura.

'I think you do. Fallon and Dick could make a lot of trouble for each other but you and I know that they have got more sense.' There had been a lot of huffing and puffing from the Army Board, she said, but the smoke and mirrors chaps in Public Relations were going to bury the whole business. The official line was that it was just an end-of-term stunt by one of the universities. 'Fallon will get his promotion but he is going to Washington. We will have a lot of fun there. Brussels isn't the place it used to be.'

Trench's career had hung in the balance for a few days. Then he took a telephone call from a field marshal.

'Trench?'

'Yes, Field Marshal.'

'Fallon Furniss told me about that problem you had with the MPs on that exercise. What you did was absolutely right. I had the same trouble in the Ardennes in '45. It almost cost us the battle. If the MPs were the genuine article, the planners should have made that clear at the outset. I have expressed my views in the strongest terms and at the highest level. Enjoy your time in Brussels. You have earned it.'

***

It was the weekend and on the early morning flight from Heathrow to Brussels, Laura and her husband had the cabin virtually to themselves.

'What does it feel like to be married to a three-star general?' Dick Trench asked with a smile.

'What does it feel like to be married to a common criminal?' countered Laura. 'Abduction, kidnapping, outraging public decency – the charge sheet is a long one. The whole thing got right out of hand. I put your career at risk. I feel thoroughly ashamed of myself.'

Dick Trench put his arm around her and they kissed. 'Being abducted by you, Laura, is much the nicest thing that has ever happened to me. So, let's leave it at that, shall we?'

Rapport

It had been a warm day. The sun was low in the sky and the scent of roses heavy on the evening air. The drone of home-going traffic from Clapham Common could be heard intermittently above the noise of conversation. Somewhere a church bell was tolling eight o'clock. The small paved garden was crowded and even limited movement was not without hazard.

Unaware of the presence of each other, indeed of the very existence of such another, they turned at the same moment like a pair of mechanical pirouettes – *and collided!*

'I'm frightfully sorry. I wasn't looking–'

'It was my fault. Really it was–'

'I have spilt your drink. Let me get–'

'Please don't bother. Neil and I must be going soon.' She brushed her fingers down the side of the cotton dress.

'Your dress–'

'It's only white wine. It will dry out quickly.'

For the first time the parties to this trifling incident raised their heads and their eyes met. They stared. It was uncanny. The same slim build, the same wide mouth, the same shade of auburn hair with its wave over the ears, even the green eyes were identical in hue.

'What … what is your name?' the young man stammered.

'Sally. Sally Bligh.'

'Mine is Simon. Simon Byrne.'

Sally sighed softly. Life was so cruel to play this trick on her now. Now that it was too late. For her, growing up had meant finding a husband, getting married and having children. It had meant accepting life with all its imperfections and learning to cultivate happiness as a good habit if one was not to make those who loved one miserable. It had meant resigning herself to the probability that the man of her dreams did not exist – or if he did, that a grudging providence was unlikely to put him in her way. And yet here she was looking at him – as if she had awakened from that dream to find him still standing there.

'How odd that we both should have got married six years ago and in the same month,' Simon heard himself saying. His mind recoiled from the possibility that the weddings might even have taken place on the same day. The thought that some tenuous covenant between them had been abrogated at the same moment was too painful to dwell upon.

This was the girl for whom he had been searching all those years. She had always seemed so close to him, so attainable, so inevitable. At drinks parties he would be sure that he would find her in the next room. In the cinema he would be certain to see her as soon as the lights came up. When the train stopped at the next station, she would be standing on the platform as if she had been waiting for him. And now here she was at last, but she had come too late.

Some movement in that throng had caught his eye. 'I'm afraid it's time that I–'

'Please don't go. I think I would die if I felt we would never meet again.'

Someone had called his name. A hand waved above the heads of the crowd.

Sally stared over Simon's shoulder. 'Does that hand belong to you?'

'I'm afraid it does.'

'Well, the curfew has sounded.' Her eyes held him.

'I can't leave you. Not like this.' Their fingers touched. Sally closed her eyes. 'I think I am going to faint.'

'You look white as a sheet. Let me get you a glass of water.'

'No, you must go. Go now.'

'*Simon!* Didn't you hear me call? You know we promised the au-pair we would be back no later than half-past eight.' There was a flash of a gold bracelet on a long brown arm, a dismissive swirl of blonde hair and Simon Byrne was led away and lost to sight.

2

At eleven o'clock on Monday morning the telephone rang on Simon's desk.

'Simon! Is that you?' a voice whispered.

'Sally!'

'Can you talk?'

Simon looked furtively down the length of the gallery. 'It's alright. My secretary has gone downstairs to make some coffee. How on earth did you get hold of me?'

'When I telephoned Priscilla to thank her for the party, she said that she had just been speaking to Ann.'

'To my wife?'

'Ann is your wife, isn't she?'

Simon passed a hand over his forehead. 'I'm sorry, Sally. I'm still trying to get my mind into gear.'

'Me too. But I had wit enough to draw Priscilla out a little and she told me that you and Ann lived in Fulham and had two children and how you ran a picture gallery, and so on. She got the name of it wrong but the man on directory enquiries was nice and traced it for me … are you still there?'

'Of course I am.'

'You are very silent.'

'That's because you have been gabbling non-stop.'

'It's nerves. Imagine my feelings. When you left I thought I had lost you for ever. The last three days have been terrible. Have they been bad for you?'

'*Unendurable*. I don't know how I have got through them. Ann thought I must be sickening for something. She wanted to call the doctor. I said it was only mild food poisoning. I blamed it on the avocado dip.'

'That was terribly unfair. The dip was delicious.'

'It was all I could think of.'

'We have to make a plan, Simon. Being away from you is like being cut in half. And when I am with Neil, it feels so odd – we are like the two halves of a pantomime horse.' She gave a little gasp of misery. 'Nothing will ever be the same again.'

'Don't cry, Sally.'

'I'm trying not to ... but can't you see that the whole thing is impossible? How can we be together? I still love Neil the way you love Ann. We couldn't bear to do anything to hurt them.'

'Sally, if this goes on, we are going to hurt them.'

'Do you think that if we met and made love–?'

'I have never cheated on Ann and I'm not starting–'

'There is no question of having an affair, Simon. I wouldn't dream of deceiving Neil.'

'But I thought you said–'

'I am suggesting that we make love – once.'

'How will that help?'

'If we make love, our chromosomes will mix. You will become part of me and I of you. That way we shall always be together.'

'It doesn't sound very scientific.'

'It's as scientific as it could be. Our chromosomes are like that glue that you buy in two little tubes and mix into a paste. It sticks like anything.'

'And then … when we have … done it … we return to our sweethearts?'

'Yes – and never look at anyone else for the rest of our lives.'

'When shall we do it?'

'We must hurry. Every day we are going to make Neil and Ann more wretched. Next weekend we can–'

'Saturdays are hopeless. The gallery is open all day.'

'What about Sunday?'

'That's no good either. I have to do things with the children.'

'What are we going to do? I'm teaching three to five year olds all week. I can't take time off.'

'When do you get home?'

'I'm always back by four.'

'Where do you live?'

'Quite near you. Hurlingham. About five minutes walk from the school.'

'How about Wednesday afternoon? The gallery has a half day.'

'Two days. It will seem like an eternity.'

'What will you do with your children?'

'I'll ask a friend to take them to the park that afternoon. She has two of her own and they all get on together.'

'Good. That's settled. I will come round to your flat no later than–'

'*You can't come here!* I should have told you. Neil works from home.'

'*From home!* Hasn't he got an office to go to?'

'He writes computer programmes. Most of those jobs are done from home these days. Supposing I came to you?'

'Not a chance. Ann is in the flat most of the day.'

'What does she do?'

'She draws and paints. Mostly illustrations for children's books.'

'We could go to a hotel. Sign the register in a false name.'

'It isn't that easy. You can't just turn up without any luggage and ask for a double bedroom.'

'We could bring a suitcase.'

'It's very risky. If Ann caught me sneaking back to the flat carrying–'

'We could buy an overnight case and leave it behind.'

'Hotels don't like clients who treat their establishment like a brothel. They give the place a bad name.'

'Oh, Simon! *Don't be so negative!* You are the man. *Think* of something!'

'There is my car. We could put the seats down.'

'Your car! I don't insist on a four-poster but I had set my heart on a bed of some sort. And fat, squashy pillows, lots of frills and flounces…'

'It won't take very long, Sally.'

'You make it sound like an emergency visit to the dentist.'

'I'm sorry, Sally, but our own comfort is not the first consideration. You seem to have forgotten that we are doing this for Neil and Ann.'

'You're right. I was being thoughtless and selfish. Let's use your car. I can bring a pillow.'

'And there's a tartan rug in the back. We shall have to find somewhere very secluded. That isn't going to be easy.'

'Simon, I have just had an inspiration. I know the perfect place. Completely deserted.'

'How long would it take to drive there?'

'No more than ten minutes from Fulham.'

They agreed to meet at four o'clock on the following Wednesday in a small side street off Fulham Broadway

3

Sally tapped urgently on the car window. 'Simon. Is that you?'

'Of course it's me.'

'Then take off those awful dark glasses and let me in.' She clambered into the seat next to him. 'I'm sorry about the long skirt.'

'It's not very sexy.'

'The headmistress doesn't like sexy schoolteachers. She says that they unsettle the fathers.'

'I know what she means.'

She gazed at him. 'You have the most beautiful eyes I have ever seen.'

'Except when you sit in front of the looking glass.'

'Flatterer.' They kissed and kissed again and she had to push him gently away. 'Now, Simon, try to behave until we get there.'

Simon started the car. 'I don't know whether I can wait that long. I think I shall explode.'

'Think about something else.'

'There isn't anything else.'

They crossed the Kings Road. 'Turn right here, Simon. Then second left … no darling, second left.'

'I'm sorry, Sally. I'm in such a state.'

Sally patted his arm. 'It won't be long now. Left again.'

Simon reached under the hem of her skirt and ran his fingers up her stockings. 'You feel delicious. Like a really exciting Christmas present – one of those mysterious ones that you feel all over trying to guess what's inside.'

'I want you to unwrap me, darling – and find out.'

'It's going to be mind-blowing.'

'Cosmic. Sharp left after the bus stop.'

'Like the first day of creation.'

'Like roller-skating down a rainbow. Right at the lights.'

Simon wrestled with his tie. 'If I get any hotter, I shall catch fire.'

Sally unfastened a button on his shirt and slipped a hand inside. 'I can feel your heart beating. Like a wild bird in a cage.' The hand moved to his knee. 'Have you saved yourself for me, Simon? Promise me you haven't made love since we met.'

'You know I wouldn't. I remembered what you said about chromosomes. Mine might get confused if I slept with Ann – and then this wouldn't work.'

Sally squeezed the knee affectionately. 'How odd that you should say that. I feel exactly the same. Neil made a pass at me after supper on Saturday night. I had to tease him out of it.'

'How did you do that?'

'We had ice cream and stem ginger for dessert. I told him it was the ginger.'

'Does ginger turn him on?'

'That and mustard pickle. Left here.'

The street in which they found themselves was a narrow cul-de-sac bounded by old warehouses. The place had a derelict appearance. The buildings were grimy and many of the windows broken.

'Is this it?' Simon asked.

'Yes. It's perfect, don't you think? Nobody works around here any more.'

'I'm not surprised.'

'The whole area is scheduled for demolition.' Sally gazed serenely about her.

Simon clutched the wheel tightly as the car bounced in and out of the potholes. 'How did you find this place?'

'By accident. Neil and I were flat hunting. We got lost.'

Simon drove to the end and parked by the side of the road. He scanned his mirror. 'All clear. Now for that *real* kiss.' He reached towards Sally and pulled her into his arms. They kissed fiercely, hungrily, revenging themselves on the long days that had kept them apart.

'It's not enough,' Sally moaned. 'I want you … I need you … all of you.' She turned and thumped with her small fists on the back of the seat.

'Not like that, Sally,' Simon muttered. 'Turn the levers on the side of the seats and the backs will go down.' His fingers were on the buttons of her blouse, his face nuzzling into the shallow hollow at the base of her neck, breathing in her warmth, the fragrance of her skin.

Sally found the levers and turned them. The seats reclined sedately by a few inches and then stopped.

'Go on,' murmured Simon. 'All the way down.'

'I can't move them–'

'Leave them to me.' Simon took over the levers. He wrestled with one seat then with the other. Neither moved. He pulled open the flap to the glove compartment.

'What are you looking for, Simon?' Sally's voice had an edge to it.

'This.' He waved the instruction manual at her.

'Why?'

'To find out how to get the seats to go down.'

'We already know the answer to that. They don't go down.'

He flicked through the pages. 'Be quiet for a moment. I want to concentrate.'

'It would have helped if you had concentrated before you bought the car.' She gnawed on a fingernail. 'How anyone could do anything so stupid I cannot imagine.'

Simon slammed the door of the glove compartment. 'I'm sorry, Sally, but it just didn't occur to me when I bought the car that I might want it for what … for what you want it for.'

'Well, think of a solution before I stop wanting it.' She stared fixedly through the windscreen, her cheeks pink with anger.

'We could open the doors and lie across the seats.'

'Is that a serious suggestion?'

'It might be a little awkward…'

'Just a little. What do we do about the gear lever between the front two seats?'

'The rear seats then?'

'You must think I am made like a caterpillar. The armrest is fixed. It will come right in the small of my back. And what am I going to do with my head? I can't leave it stuck out in the road.'

'We could use the jack – put it under your neck. That might help.'

'If you can't be serious you can drive me home.'

Simon stared gloomily into the floor well. 'I suppose I could kneel down there–'

'With your feet between the pedals? That would be ecstatic.'

Simon chuckled. 'Where's your sense of humour, Sally?'

'It's not funny, Simon. *It's tragic.* If you can't see that then I think we have both made a *terrible* mistake.' Tears of anger and frustration pricked at her eyes.

There came a cry from behind them. A group of small boys in shorts and grubby jerseys ran around the corner kicking a football between them.

'That's all we need,' Simon growled. He started the car.

'Where are you going now?' Sally sniffled miserably.

'I think we should go home.' There was an infuriated screech of tyres as he reversed and drove back up the road.

'Oh, Simon. I'm so unhappy. It was all going to be so perfect and now everything's horrid.'

'It's my fault.'

'Yes it is, but we will get it right next time. *There's no need to look so savage.*'

'*How do you expect me to look*? Frustration is very bad for a man. It can make one quite ill.'

'Stop moaning. It's just as bad for me.'

'My chromosomes feel very odd. As if they have gone tearing off to the airport only to find that the flight has just been cancelled.' He put his foot down and the car picked up speed.

The boys scurried towards them kicking the football on ahead.

'Watch out for the children, Simon!'

'Shut up! I'm nowhere near them.'

There was a slight bump. *'Stop! You have hit something!'* cried Sally in alarm.

Simon braked sharply. The boys were abreast of them, shouting and gesticulating. He wound down his window. 'What's the trouble?'

A chorus of wails greeted him. They were pointing at the car. The tallest of them put his head in at the window. 'Mister,' he said reproachfully, 'can we have our ball back?'

'I haven't got your ball,' replied Simon irritably.

'Simon, do be nice to them.'

'Why should I be nice to them? I don't like being accused of something I haven't done – especially by this crowd of ragamuffins.'

'*Oh, Simon, don't be so pompous!*. Get out of the car and help them find their ball.'

Reluctantly Simon clambered out. Ten small faces gazed up at him, waiting for him to speak. 'Now where is this ball you say that I have taken?'

'You run over it, Mister,' exclaimed their leader. The cry was taken up by his mates. One of the urchins dived under the car.

'*Come out!*' He grabbed at the boy's ankles and pulled him back.

It took Simon ten minutes to retrieve the ball and as long again for Sally to wipe the oil smears from his face.

'You've burned yourself, you poor darling.' She raised his hand to her lips and kissed the livid scorch mark.

'I must have touched the exhaust pipe.'

'You were so kind, so brave. I was very proud of you.'

'At least they are happy,' said Simon, his mood lifting a little. Looking in his rear mirror he could see the football match in full swing. They drove slowly back in silence.

'Today was a test,' Sally said at last. 'A test of our resolve. Tomorrow–'

'Tomorrow is no good,' Simon said sharply. 'You seem to have forgotten that I have a business to run.'

Sally took his hand and laid it against her cheek. 'Simon, we *have* to make love tomorrow. You *must* see that. We owe it to Ann and Neil. We can't leave things like this. Our marriages are falling apart.'

'I will try to get away early.'

'Of course you can. What's the point of being the boss if–'

'Alright. I will be at the same place at four fifteen.'

'Where shall we go?'

'This time I will choose.'

'I know it is going to be perfect.'

4

'Richmond Park! *What a brilliant idea!*' Sally bounced up and down with excitement as they drove through the gates. 'Sunlit glades, shady arbours…'

'And us,' Simon reminded her.

'And us,' Sally echoed. She ruffled his hair where it curled at the nape of the neck. Close to the ponds they found a car park. Simon took the travelling rug and, linking hands, they went on foot, following a sandy track across the heath.

'Let's try there.' Sally led the way between low bracken to a small clearing under a large oak tree. 'Isn't this wonderful, Simon?'

Shading his eyes with his hand, Simon scanned the terrain. 'It's perfect. There's nobody in sight.' He spread the rug on the ground.

'It's better than perfect. It's sublime.' Sally kicked off her shoes. 'It's the moment I have been dreaming about ever since I first saw you.' Throwing herself down on the rug, she stretched her arms up to him. 'Make love to me, Simon…'

Simon tore off his jacket and tie and knelt beside her. 'Now for that kiss…'

'No, not like that,' she murmured. 'Come closer. I want to feel you against me.' She pulled him down beside her. 'I want to feel all the wonderful bits of you, the soft places and the hard places…'

'The curves and the hollows…' he muttered feverishly, his fingers already on the buttons of her blouse.

Their lips met in a scalding kiss. Her fingers were at his shirt buttons, running over his chest, pushing the collar away from his neck. His heart was hammering, the blood was beating in his ears, his body was simmering as if it was being heated in a pressure cooker.

'Sally, darling…' His hand felt for the zipper of her long skirt, running it down in short, jerky movements. 'At last … together … really together.'

'Oh, Simon … it's going to be so beautiful…'

'I want you, Sally … you'll never know … how much…'

'Show me … my love…' She raised her body, allowing him to draw the skirt down over her hips, sliding it over her thighs and down her long slim legs. With an impatient movement she shuffled the garment off her feet. Her hands reached for the buckle of his belt. 'Show me … darling … show me how much…'

'Over here, Miss Vickers!' The piercing treble of a child's voice.

They sat bolt upright, the heat draining from their bodies as if a pail of water had been thrown over them. Sally grabbed at her skirt. Simon fiddled feverishly with his shirt buttons.

No more than thirty yards away a troop of schoolchildren, led by their teacher, was coming down the track. They were a mixture of boys and girls in short-sleeved shirts and corduroy shorts. In their hands they carried small notepads.

'A nature ramble,' said Simon bitterly. 'Why can't they go and look for a rabbit's dropping or a pigeon feather somewhere else?'

'With the whole park to choose from ... why ... why ... why ... do they have to spoil everything for us?' Sally blinked away an infuriated tear.

The schoolmistress was pointing at something on the ground. 'Well done, Penelope. That's a roe deer's print. The rest of you gather around and make a drawing in your notebooks.'

At that moment, one of the children cried out, 'Look, Miss Vickers! *A squirrel*!'

The cry was taken up. 'A squirrel! A squirrel! *We want to see the squirrel*.'

With a sinking feeling in his stomach, Simon peered upwards. A squirrel was leaping from branch to branch in the foliage above their heads. He risked a peep over the top of the bracken. 'Sally! *Quick!* We shall have to make a dash for it. They are coming straight for us.' He picked up his jacket and, bending low, scurried off through the undergrowth.

'*Wait for me, Simon!* I must put on my skirt.'

'There isn't time,' he called over his shoulder.

'My shoes! *I must put on my shoes!*'

'Never mind your shoes.' Then he heard her cry out. '*Help me, Simon*!'

He stopped and turned around. 'Where are you?'

He found Sally, scarlet cheeked, her satin pants stained with green, sitting disconsolately among the broken stems. 'I think I must have twisted my ankle.' She screwed up her eyes in pain.

Simon stared down at her. There was a sour taste in his mouth as if something was curdling inside him. 'Take my hand,' he said brusquely. 'Try to get up.'

She looked up at him, her eyes brimming with tears. 'I can't. It hurts too much.'

'We must try to go a little further.' He reached under her arms and tried to raise her.

She tried to support her weight on the injured foot. 'It hurts dreadfully, Simon.' She sank back onto the ground. 'Let me rest for a while.'

She looked so sweet, so desirable, lying there, Simon thought. Surely something could be made of this setback. His chromosomes were in no mood for a second disappointment. Making swimming movements with his arms, he created a small island in the green sea that engulfed them. 'Don't worry, Sally. Nobody can see us.'

'Are the children coming this way?'

'No. We are quite safe.' He looked around for the rug. 'Where is the rug?'

'I'm sorry. In the panic I forgot it.'

He grimaced. 'Well, we can't go back for it now.'

Sally lay back and closed her eyes. The sun was warm on her face. 'I must look a perfect sight.'

'To me you look perfectly lovely.' He folded the skirt and placed it under her head as a pillow. With the tip of his finger he stroked the drowsy eyelids with their long, dark, curling lashes. He gazed down at her, watching the colour come and go in her cheeks, the delicate quivering of her nostrils with every soft intake of breath, the exuberant ripeness pressing at the constraints of her blouse. With the tip of her tongue she moistened her lips. 'You are so sweet, Simon,' she sighed. 'So understanding.'

He could resist her no longer. He bent down and kissed her. And threw off his shirt. His trousers followed.

'You are very busy suddenly,' she murmured. She opened an eye. 'Have you forgotten that I am an invalid?'

'Try to relax, darling,' he breathed in her ear. 'I am going to give you something to make you better.' His hands glided up her legs to the wide French tops of her stockings and he rolled them down.

A tremor ran through her body. 'You have the most beautiful eyes, Simon … they do the oddest things to me…'

'What sort of things?' he whispered.

'I'm melting inside. Like a strawberry ice cream in the hot sun.' She shifted her position, tautening the shiny triangle of satin under his eyes. Through the embroidered lacework he caught a glimpse of pale, peach-coloured skin.

Her lips trembled. 'This remedy you mentioned…'

'I have the prescription with me.' Simon undid the buttons on her blouse and slipped his hands under her to release the fastening on her bra. His fingers moved swiftly to the waistband of her pants.

'Simon … *listen…*'

'I can't stop now, Sally.'

'There's a noise … a drumming … in my ears…' she struggled to raise herself.

'And in mine, darling.' He pressed her down again.

'*Stop it, Simon!*' She slid from under him.

With a curse Simon raised his head. 'It's only a woman on a horse.' He drew in a furious gulp of air. 'Forget her. She can't see us.'

'Are you sure? It sounds so close.'

The horsewoman, riding hat crammed hard down on her head, was riding a large bay horse at a steady canter down a track hidden from them by the bracken.

'She has passed. Now let's get on–'

'*Wait!* What's that rustling sound? There's something in the bracken. It's coming this way.'

'Nonsense. You are imagining–'

'I tell you I can hear it. Some animal…'

Simon followed the direction of her eyes. The tops of the bracken were waving gently. 'I can hear it now … something panting…'

'Oh, Simon … *hold me!* I'm frightened.'

Wide-eyed with apprehension, they huddled together, their arms wound about each other like the Babes in the Wood.

No more than a few feet from them the fronds parted and a pair of black eyes looked out at them.

'*What is it*?' Sally gasped. She shrank behind Simon's shoulder.

'I don't know.' He picked up a shoe and hurled it.

There was a commotion in the foliage. The eyes vanished.

'*Thank God!* It's gone!'

The eyes reappeared. Sally gave a shriek of despair.

The creature, probably mistaking this for a belated cry of welcome, gave a rapturous yelp and bounded out from its hiding place.

'*Simon! Help! Do something*!' She flailed out with her sound leg.

'*Go away, you bloody animal*!' he shouted, waving his arms to and fro.

The dog backed away but no more than a foot or two. It stood motionless, regarding them reproachfully, its tongue lolling, a puzzled frown furrowing the glossy black brow.

Simon regretted his ill manners. It was a Labrador. The gentleman of the canine race. 'He doesn't mean any harm. He wants to play. He's only a young dog.'

'I don't care if he was born ten minutes ago. I don't want him near me.' Stealthily she stretched out an arm and started to pull her skirt towards her.

The dog, muzzle lowered, watched her, ready to participate in whatever new game was being devised for its entertainment.

Sally's nerve broke. She gave the skirt a sharp tug. The dog leaped, landing at her feet. It feinted this way and that looking for an opening. *'Simon!'* she cried out, close to panic. *'Get the brute off me!'*

Encumbered by having one hand engaged in holding up his trousers, Simon grabbed at the dog and missed. 'It's only trying to make friends. Let it lick your hands.'

'It's done that! *Now it's trying to lick me all over*!' She raised her hands to fend off the dog, relaxing her hold on the skirt. The creature saw its chance. Snatching the skirt between its jaws, it whirled around and plunged into the undergrowth.

'My skirt!' shrieked Sally. *'Come back with my skirt!'*

'Stop shouting, Sally! And get down. You can't rush around the park in your pants. You will get us arrested.'

Sally hobbled a step or two. 'Run after it, Simon,' she moaned. 'I can't. My ankle is killing me.' She collapsed on the ground and put her head in her hands.

Simon thrust his feet into his shoes, picked up his shirt and set off through the bracken. Coming to a broad track, he saw that the horse and rider had stopped. The dog was loping along to rejoin his mistress, trailing its booty through the dust.

Some moments later, dishevelled and breathless from his exertions, Simon found himself staring up at the lady on the horse. She had a pair of piercing blue eyes separated by a beaky nose. Under a dusting of powder, her complexion was a network of fine crimson lines.

Simon pointed at the dog. 'Your dog has taken something belonging to us.' His sense of grievance was undermined by an uneasy feeling that the animal had been a witness to a serious breach of a local byelaw.

'Us?' The woman looked about her. 'Are there two of you?'

'My friend is over there somewhere.' Simon's hand drifted vaguely over the ocean of green bracken. 'She fell over and twisted her ankle.'

'Indeed. I hope she is not badly hurt.'

'She will be better after a little rest. She is probably lying down.'

'That seems very sensible in the circumstances. Are you sure I cannot help in any way?'

Simon thanked her. No, he assured her, they could manage. 'If you could help me get … our things back, I won't trouble you any more.'

'*Shako*!' the woman pointed her whip at the dog. 'What have you been up to?' Shako wagged his tail but gave no other indication that he was prepared to negotiate.

Forcing his features into an ingratiating smile, Simon bent down and held out his hand. 'Good boy. Come along now.'

The woman called sharply to the dog. '*Shako!* Return the gentleman's property. Drop it! *At once*!' She slapped her boot with the hunting crop.

After a few moments of token resistance the dog surrendered its spoils. The woman watched curiously as Simon hastily rolled the garment into a bundle and tucked it under his arm.

'I don't wish to pry, but that looks very much like a woman's skirt.'

'It is,' Simon admitted. 'We used it as a rug. A picnic rug,' he added in some confusion.

'What an ingenious arrangement.' The woman took up the reins. 'But I do think you should encourage your friend to put her rug back on before she leaves the park.' She tapped the horse with her heels, called to the dog and trotted away.

5

It was almost a week later. For six long days of mutual anguish there had been no communication between them. A little after four o'clock on the Wednesday afternoon, Simon drove his car to the side street off Fulham Broadway. Sally was already there, staring blindly into the window of a shop that sold bicycle parts.

She leaped into the car. 'Simon, darling. I wasn't sure you would be here.' She brushed away a tear with her hand.

'After what happened last week I was afraid we might never see each other again.'

Sally pressed her fingers to his lips. 'It will never be mentioned again.'

'How is the ankle?'

'Mended.'

'And the skirt?'

'It was ruined. I had to throw it out. Neil didn't see me come in, thank heavens. He had gone to the post office.'

'How are things with Neil?'

'*Dreadful!* He says I have been behaving so oddly. He is sure there is something wrong with me.'

'I had a frightful row with Ann. She thinks I ought to go and see a psychiatrist.'

'I feel so terribly sorry for both of them. What we are putting them through is awful.'

'It will all come right, you'll see. After today everything will be different.'

They kissed. Sally ran her hands over the shoulders of his suede jacket. 'Those wonderful muscles … what a treat they are in for … just thinking about it makes me go hot and cold all over.'

Simon stared at the curves of her body moulded by the tight-fitting navy-blue dress with its bold white polka dots. 'Are you wearing anything under that, Sally?'

She giggled. 'That's for you to find out.'

'Looking at you makes me feel quite dizzy.' He took a deep breath, unfastened the top button of his shirt and loosened his tie.

They drove to the river, following the embankment and then crossed Lambeth Bridge. Simon squeezed her hand. 'Today is going to be very special.'

'The day we skated down the rainbow.'

'The day we climbed the Magic Mountain.'

'The day–' she glanced into the back of the car. 'Where did you get the suitcase?' It was a sorry-looking object, the leather scuffed and one of the straps missing.

'I bought it at the lost property office.'

'It looks as if the owner lost it on purpose.'

'I didn't think it should look too new.' They turned into a narrow street.

'Where are we going?' She cast a dismal eye at the long terrace of drab grey houses. In the distance, the rust-streaked lines of a gasometer could be seen against a lowering sky.

'A private hotel. It was advertised in the local paper.'

'I hope it is respectable. This area around Waterloo Station isn't very salubrious.'

'Don't worry. I spoke to the manager. He said that it was a family-run hotel – the sort of place that people go to if they are travelling later in the day and need a base for a few hours.'

'You are clever, Simon.'

The car slowed and pulled in to the kerb. 'How about that, Sally? What better omen could we have? A vacant parking space and two hours left on the meter.'

'Two hours of bliss.'

'One hundred and twenty minutes of ecstasy.'

'Do you think it matters if we enjoy it so much? We are doing it for Ann and Neil. It would spoil everything if I felt that we were just being selfish.'

'If it wasn't wonderful, our chromosomes wouldn't interact – and that would be a disaster.'

'Are you sure?'

'Absolutely.'

'I love it when a man takes charge. It is so reassuring.' Sally put her arm under his jacket, strumming her fingers lightly up and down his ribcage. 'You do look funny carrying that battered old suitcase,' she said teasingly.

Simon tightened his arm about her waist. 'I must look like a tramp going on honeymoon.'

They climbed the steep flight of steps that led to the hotel entrance. The front was freshly painted in a bright dandelion yellow. A defective mauve neon sign above the door provided travellers with fitful reminders that they had arrived at the Paradise Hotel. A sign in the window advertised, *Rooms Available by the Hour*.

Sally paused on the top step. She held on to Simon's hand. 'Are you sure this place is alright, Simon?'

'Of course I'm sure. Pay no attention to first impressions. They can be so misleading.'

'I wish someone had told me that two weeks ago.'

'What do you mean by that?' Simon swung her around to face him.

'Oh, Simon, don't be so touchy. I was only joking.'

He forced a smile. 'It wasn't a very good joke. For a moment I thought–'

'Let's go in, darling. *Please…*'

There was a counter at the end of a dimly lit lobby with a row of pigeonholes above for keys. Simon pushed a bell button. They could hear a door being opened. He wrinkled his nose.

'What's that horrible smell?'

'Cooking oil.'

The man who appeared in answer to the summons was of swarthy complexion and wearing a collarless shirt under a loose-fitting maroon waistcoat which flapped about his short, thickset body. A shred of spaghetti hung from the corner of his heavy black moustache. The finger that he pointed at Simon was yellow with nicotine. 'I am Mr Malik, the manager. Are you the gentleman who telephoned?'

'Yes. I reserved a double bedroom … for two hours. As I told you, my wife and I are only in London for the day.' Tentatively, Simon raised and lowered the suitcase in the hope that production of new evidence would add substance to this statement.

'Minimum four hours,' said Mr Malik impassively. He found a torn envelope in the waste-paper basket, licked the end of his pencil and laboriously wrote out a bill.

'But you said–'

'Let's not argue, Simon,' Sally interjected. 'Let's just get on with it.'

'Quicker you pay – quicker you get on with it,' agreed Mr Malik without raising his head.

'Very well,' said Simon resignedly. He passed a number of notes to the manager who added them to a thick, greasy wad which appeared briefly from a back trouser pocket. The man reached behind him for a key. 'Number seventy-five. On the seventh floor. Very excellent room. Many fine appointments.' His hand went under the counter and he pulled out a small brass bell. 'Pomeroy will show you to your room.'

'We are perfectly capable of finding our own way, thank you,' said Simon stiffly.

'Pomeroy is helping you,' said Mr Malik. 'Pomeroy is helping everybody.' He tinkled the bell.

Sally folded her arms tightly against herself. Her voice trembled with suppressed fury.

'*Who* exactly *is* Pomeroy, Mr Malik?'

'Pomeroy very fine overseas gentleman. Mature student in hotel management. City and Guilds.' He tinkled the bell vigorously.

A middle-aged man with a face as black as ebony and grizzled grey hair emerged from behind a bead curtain. The silk facings on his crumpled dinner jacket were green with age. His trousers were gathered at the ankles and the impression that he might have been wearing the lower half of a tracksuit was strengthened by the trainers on his feet. As he listened to his instructions, he made final adjustments to a frayed bow tie before taking the key from the manager and picking up the suitcase. 'Floor seven. Much walking. Pomeroy lead the way.'

They followed Pomeroy up the stairs. At one time there must have been a carpet and stair rods but only the brass runners remained as a reminder of past glories. It was a warm day with a hint of thunder in the air and many of the bedroom doors were open. Sleeping forms could be seen slumped against the walls or curled up on mattresses that had spilled out into the corridors. The air reverberated with the throb of rap music. An old man in a turban was squatting on a bathroom floor cooking curry over a primus stove. Somewhere a baby was bawling. A heavily built youth in a black bomber jacket with an Alsatian dog on a lead ran past them on the stairs. Two boys in ragged jeans were playing football with an empty beer can.

'Much coming and going,' said Pomeroy.

'I think we should get out of this place,' said Sally through clenched teeth.

Simon took her arm. 'Hang on, Sally. We are nearly there.'

'Happy times soon,' said Pomeroy. His forehead glistened with perspiration and he stopped on a landing to rest for a moment.

'Who are all these people ... staying in the hotel?' Simon asked with breathless exasperation.

'Many guests from overseas,' replied Pomeroy.

'Do they have to pay for their rooms?' Simon pursued, prompted by a nagging suspicion that the guests might be enjoying the hospitality of the Paradise Hotel on terms denied to him.

'All on welfare. Local authority pays,' said Pomeroy in his deep voice. 'Rule Britannia,' he added as if to dispel any doubt as to the legitimacy of the arrangement.

They resumed their climb. Pomeroy steered his charges around the frame of a wheel-less bicycle chained to a radiator. 'Go careful here,' he warned them. 'People on this floor no like strangers. Sometime bad things happen.'

'What sort of bad things?' asked Sally. She peered anxiously down a corridor that a number of teenage boys had converted to a skittle alley.

'They hear visitors coming up. Sometime they roll supermarket trolley down stairs. No make good impression.'

To their relief they reached the seventh floor without incident and stopped in front of a bedroom door. The woodwork was splintered as if it had resisted a number of attempts at forcible entry. 'No one on this floor – everyone leave early this morning. All tranquil.' Pomeroy pushed the key into the lock. 'Now you have happy time.'

Simon felt in his pocket for a coin. 'Thank you, Pomeroy. We can manage–'

'We shall want something to drink,' Sally broke in. 'Can you bring us a bottle of mineral water?'

'No minerals.' Pomeroy pronounced. He pushed open the door. 'Very fine Cuban beer. I bring it to you after yoyo.'

'After–?'

'Leave it, Sally,' Simon said quickly. They stood in silence looking around the room, at the small double bed with its threadbare coverlet in faded coral, the stained and peeling wallpaper, the cracked washbasin, the ceiling from which a naked light bulb hung by a metal chain. Through dingy net curtains they could dimly perceive an expanse of grey wall and a large ducting pipe from which thin plumes of vapour rose at irregular intervals. Simon turned to Pomeroy with a despairing gesture. 'Is this the best you can do?'

'Very best room,' Pomeroy replied, nodding his head emphatically. 'Other rooms not up to quality.'

Simon shrugged resignedly. 'Alright, I suppose we have no choice. But we must have something that we can drink.'

'Cuban beer for the gentleman. Mango juice for the lady.' Pomeroy found a pen and made a note on the palm of his hand.

'Is that all?'

'You like it. Very 'vigorating. After refreshment you go two time yoyo.'

'My wife and I are here to rest for an hour or so before catching the train,' said Simon severely. He extracted a coin from the pocket of his trousers and passed it to Pomeroy.

Pomeroy's dark eyes rolled up and down like counters in a gaming machine before coming to rest on the small coin. 'Room service five pounds. Special offer.' He searched in his pockets for a scrap of paper. 'If you like I make you a bill.'

Sally sat down carefully on the bed. The springs creaked like a rusty hinge. 'Give Pomeroy his five pounds, Simon – or we shall be arguing here all day.'

Pomeroy nodded. 'Sooner you pay Pomeroy, sooner you have happy time.' He took the note from Simon and stuffed it into his breast pocket. From the recesses of his clothing he retrieved a tobacco tin and started to roll himself a cigarette.

Sally took a deep breath. 'Pomeroy, you have been very helpful but my husband and I would now like to be left alone.'

Pomeroy licked the edge of the cigarette paper, pressed it into position and slotted the finished product behind his ear. 'Pomeroy feel very tender to young people,' he said confidingly. 'Not easy find safe place to have yoyo.' He went to the wardrobe door and swung it open. 'Mirror behind door. You go to bed. You do yoyo. You see everything. No extra charge. Very fine appointment.' He rummaged inside, pulled out a metal coat hanger and ran his finger down the struts to remove the dust. 'When you want room service, you strike hanger on fire escape outside window. Pomeroy hear you. Pomeroy helping with everything.'

'Thank you, Pomeroy–'

'Pomeroy going now. Pomeroy thinking of you having happy time.' The door closed behind him.

'Sally, I'm sorry, but how could I imagine–'

Sally tossed the coverlet off the bed and threw back the duvet. 'Help me out of this dress, Simon.'

'Sally, what a sport you are. I have never loved you more than I do at this–'

'Tell me later, Simon. Hurry up.' In a fever of impatience she waited while his fingers scampered down the buttons. She pulled the dress over her head.

'Sally! You aren't wearing a bra!' Simon gasped. He tossed jacket, shirt, tie and socks onto a chair.

'I thought you deserved a treat after all the disappointments that you have had.'

He took her in his arms. 'I can't quite believe this is happening.'

'Darling Simon. Simon with the beautiful eyes.' Sally stood on the tips of her toes and kissed his eyelids. 'I want to be naked under those wonderful eyes, admired by them, loved by them, possessed by them.' She ran her hand down his back to the waistband of his boxer shorts. 'Make it happen, Simon. Make it happen now.' She pulled him down onto the bed.

He gazed at her hungrily. 'I want to kiss you from the crown of your head to the tip of your toes.'

Sally tossed her head from side to side, flailing his cheeks with her hair. 'No darling. I want you now. All of you … now.' She slid his shorts down over his rump. 'Simon, darling … I want yoyo…'

Simon's blood was running like a mill race. 'Oh, Sally … my love … at last … an end to hoping … to longing…' He tugged at her briefs, 'It's going to be exquisite…'

'Don't close your eyes, darling … I want to watch them when you…'

Over their heads there came the sound of scurrying feet. Then shouting. The light bulb swayed from side to side. Small flakes of plaster dropped from the ceiling.

'Simon! *Wait!* I have–'

'I'm not going to stop, Sally. Not this time. There could be an earthquake for all I care.' The rumbling grew louder. People were running down the stairs.

'You *must* stop. I have something in my eye.'

'Sally … this is torture…'

'I'm sorry but I *must* get it out … I can't concentrate while it's there.'

The feet were scuttling past their door. There was a sound of voices raised in panic. Somewhere a dog was barking excitedly.

Sally rolled from under him. 'What's all that shouting about? Is the place on fire?' She raised her head to listen.

'They can burn the hotel to the ground … this time you and I are going all the way…' He pressed her down again.

The door burst open. A young man in a tracksuit with a baseball cap on his head charged across the room, threw up the window and disappeared through it. A stream of fugitives followed, leaving in their wake belongings abandoned in haste or proving too unwieldy to negotiate the window opening. As the motley collection scuttled past them, Simon and Sally huddled together in mute stupefaction, the duvet pulled up to their chins.

One woman was carrying a baby, another driving her children in front of her like a farmer's wife with a gaggle of recalcitrant geese. The supermarket trolley made its appearance, shuttling to and fro across the room piled high with blankets, tins of food, an old electric fire and other oddments.

The last of the stragglers, a scrawny youth with a long ponytail tied up in a rubber band, paused to push a bottle of spirits into the recesses of his bedroll.

'*What the hell's happening?*' Simon bawled, his voice returning to him.

'There's a raid on,' the man replied with the imperturbability of a veteran of many past engagements. 'Social Security Investigations Unit. Take my advice and scarper while you still can.'

There was a clatter of feet on the metal fire escape as he disappeared from sight. Simon hobbled to the window, pulling up his trousers as he did so. 'They won't come in here, will they?' he called plaintively after the retreating figure.

'I wouldn't bet on it. Not unless you want to spend the rest of the day answering questions and having your picture taken.'

Tears were running down Sally's cheeks. She hurled the duvet onto the floor to join the chaotic jumble with which the room was strewn. 'I'm not moving from here, Simon,' she wailed. 'Not this time. They will have to cart me off to prison first.' She locked her arms around her knees.

Simon rushed back to the bed and pulled on the rest of his clothes. 'We daren't be caught here. *Just think*! Having our names taken, our addresses, photographs – as if we were criminals!'

They could hear footsteps mounting the stairs, Mr Malik's voice, pleading and threatening by turns.

'*Come on, Sally!*' Simon tugged her to her feet.

'Then help me into my dress.'

'*Hurry!* They are searching the rooms.'

'My buttons–'

'*Damn the buttons!* We haven't time.'

'My stockings–'

He snatched them from her. 'You can put them on later.'

The rain was spitting against the panes. Simon climbed through the window and stepped onto the fire escape.

Sally sat on the ledge. 'I'm not going down there, Simon. It's not safe.'

'*You must!* Any moment now–'

'You go first.'

A huge clap of thunder put an end to further prevarication. Grasping the rusty rails, they made a tottering descent in a steady downpour. Far below them they could see the last of the runaways before rain obscured them and they were absorbed into the drab twilight of the metropolis.

6

After the debacle of the Paradise Hotel, there had been no communication between them for ten days and then Sally telephoned Simon at the gallery. On the notice board of her local library she had seen a card advertising the Entente Marriage Guidance Clinic.

'I was desperate, Simon. I was making Neil so unhappy. I telephoned the Clinic and asked them to send me a brochure. I have it here. They specialise in PST. Guess what those letters stand for?'

'I haven't the faintest idea.'

'Psycho-Sexual Therapy. The normal course is eight one-hour sessions. Fifteen minutes of theory followed by three-quarters of an hour of practicals.'

'*Practicals!* You mean that they–'

'Listen. The final practicals lead up to a full and loving union. It says so in the brochure.'

'*Brilliant!* All we have to do is to register as a couple who are having problems in bed. Sally, you are a genius. Where is this wonderful place?'

'In Hammersmith. Only a short ride by Underground. We can meet there.'

'Is it expensive?'

'Not if we do the Accelerated Learning Course. Sessions Five and Eight.'

'*Great*! Let's sign up right away.'

'What name shall we register in?'

'Use my mother's maiden name. Glanding. We are Mr and Mrs Simon Glanding. Invent an address. There won't be any bills. I will pay by cash in advance.'

Sally completed the registration form for both of them and they met on the following Wednesday at the

Entente Clinic. It was an unremarkable red-brick building in a quiet terrace. The receptionist, a pleasant Indian girl, showed them into the sitting room, returning a few moments later with two cups of tea and a questionnaire for each of them to complete.

'How on earth do I answer the third question?' Simon asked anxiously.

Sally put a finger to her lips. 'We are on our honour not to compare notes,' she whispered. She pointed to the instructions at the top of the form.

'How satisfying is your physical relationship?' Simon muttered, reading from the form.

'Keep as close as you can to the facts or we shall get in a dreadful muddle.'

'I feel like saying that the whole thing has been a catastrophe.'

'Then say so,' Sally hissed at him.

Simon wrote busily for a few minutes before raising his head once more. 'Question Nine. "When did you last enjoy a climax with your spouse?" I have never enjoyed a climax with you.'

'Don't be such an idiot. You can't possibly say that. On the registration form I said we had two children. Where did they come from if you didn't climax?'

'I see what you mean. But how–'

'You will have to invent a date,' said Sally with exasperation. 'Otherwise they will make us do the whole dreary course.'

'Date of last climax…' Simon scratched his head and then picked up his pen.

Sally leaned over to see what he had written. 'That's back in March.'

'Yes. It's Mothering Sunday.'

'Why then?'

'I thought it looked quite plausible.'

'I suppose I'm being frightfully dim but I can't see the connection.'

'It will have to do. What about the next question? "Use an imaginative metaphor to describe the height of sexual experience."'

'Oh, Simon … you can do that … it's like climbing to the top of Mount Everest with a full orchestra playing Wagner … standing on top of the world…'

'May I use that?'

'No. That's what I have written. You mustn't copy me.'

'I could say that it's like a firework party in the rain when none of the rockets light up.'

'Poor darling. I hope that isn't true.'

No sooner had they put down their pens than they heard their names called. 'Sally and Simon?' A large woman appeared in the doorway. She had full red lips and glossy black hair chopped below the ears. She spoke with a slight accent which they found hard to place. 'Good afternoon. I am Donna. I shall be your counsellor for these two sessions. Please bring your forms and come with me.'

Their counsellor led the way down a narrow corridor, her hair scything this way and that like the disc of a power drill. As she walked, her white satin dress with its clusters of plump red cherries stretched tight and shiny over her powerful haunches. They passed through a series of interconnecting rooms to a sitting room comfortably furnished with easy chairs around a coffee table. On the walls were pictures of young people with windswept hair and wide, ecstatic smiles cantering their horses through the surf or strolling hand in hand under palm trees in the moonlight. Idyllic couples, Simon assumed, doing idyllic things in idyllic places.

They shook hands. She looked from one to the other. 'I could almost have taken you for twins you are so alike. The green eyes are particularly striking. Was it this that brought you together?'

'In a way,' replied Sally. She bit into her lip to suppress a nervous giggle.

'How interesting. Now, make yourselves comfortable while I read through your questionnaires.'

They sat in silence until she removed her heavy, horn-rimmed spectacles, laid down the papers and leaned forward. 'Sally and Simon, your relationship is drifting into crisis. I would have preferred it if you had enrolled for the full course. There are a lot of things that need to be put right.'

'I think Sessions Five and Eight will do the trick,' said Simon resolutely. The businessman in him was still awaiting some reassurance that he would get fair value for the not inconsiderable fees that he had incurred.

'I am a counsellor, not a conjuror,' Donna retorted, her mouth tightening. 'Simon, you particularly have a lot of work to do if you genuinely wish to satisfy your partner.'

'*I have*?' Simon exclaimed hotly. 'Why pick on me?'

'I am not picking on you, Simon. But we must make a start somewhere and at the Entente Clinic we start with *Attitude*. Look at the way you are sitting. At the first hint of criticism you cocked your head on one side, slumped down in your chair, stretched out your legs and waggled your feet.'

'*What's wrong with that*?' Simon burst out.

'More or less everything. The signals that you are sending are not encouraging. Had you attended the Foundation Sessions, you would know what I mean. *Body Language* is covered in Session Two. *Vocal Intonation* and *Speech Voice Pattern* are dealt with in Session Four. We must learn not to distance ourselves from our difficulties – and not to raise our voice when we are in disagreement.'

'*Well!*' said Simon. He sat rigidly in his chair, his shoulders hunched, his fingers drumming on the arms.

Sally took his hand. 'Please don't scowl like that, Simon. Try to be co-operative, darling. Donna is only trying to help us.'

Donna smiled at Sally, her large brown eyes melting like chocolates left in the sun. 'Sally is sending some very nice messages, Simon. Did you notice how she used her whole body when she spoke, her lips shaping themselves like a kiss, her hands stretched out to take yours? How she seemed to open her heart to you?'

Simon glowered at her but remained silent.

Donna patted Sally's hand. 'We must teach Simon a whole new language. Humility, a willingness to learn and to respond. That is the grammar of communication.' She collected the papers from the table and rose to her feet. 'I am going to leave you for a few minutes so that I can prepare the *Activity* area. I will meet you in *Information & Communication*. Please follow the signs to *Dysfunction* and then take the door to the left.' She spoke a few words to Sally in a low voice, nodded at her with some deliberation and left the room.

Simon frowned. 'I heard that.'

'I don't think you were meant to.'

'Well I did. What did she mean by whispering, "We are going to have to civilise the pianist?"'

'Penis, you ass – not pianist. It's that mid-Atlantic accent.'

Simon grabbed Sally's arm. '*Civilise it*! What … what do you think … she's going to do?' he stuttered.

'How do I know? Anyway, you should be pleased. It shows that we are getting somewhere.'

'But where?' muttered Simon apprehensively. He tightened the belt on his trousers and followed Sally through the door.

'This reminds me of the dentist,' said Sally with a shudder. She glanced from the examination couch to the table laid out with tubes, syringes and shiny instruments.

'Come and look at these,' said Simon. He pointed to a line of photographs with a sign underneath which read *Special Problems*. 'There is a picture of a man making love to a soda siphon.'

'Hurry up, Simon. Let's try to solve our own problems.'

Information & Communication was rather like a school classroom with a row of desks and chairs, a blackboard on a platform and charts around the walls. On a low dais beside the platform there were life-size models of a naked man and a woman in shiny white latex.

Donna bustled in to find them staring up at the two figures. 'So, you have discovered our two lovers,' she said briskly. 'We call them Mars and Venus. They are used for exercises in *Sensate Focus*.' She pointed to two small panels in stainless steel on the base. 'Look at the panels, Simon, and tell me what you see.'

'Each has three numbered buttons.'

'Correct. Now, can either of you tell me what those buttons are for?'

They both stared at her blankly.

'No ideas? And yet it should be obvious. If I press button One, Mars's primary erogenous zone will light up. *There!* It turns a sort of dull rhubarb. Now I shall press the same button for Venus and you will see that we get an exciting raspberry tint at the apex of the thighs. Button Two identifies the secondary zones. See – an enticing peachy glow on Venus's lips and over her breasts.'

'What happens if you press the third button?' asked Simon.

'That would be much too easy,' Donna replied sharply. 'It would show you the remaining zones – so often and so sadly neglected. These you must discover for yourselves.' From the pocket of her dress she produced an envelope. 'I have here a number of coloured dots. Rose pink for Sally, blue for Simon. In *Activity* you will seek out these other centres of sensation and mark each with a coloured dot. We shall then return here and compare the results with the models.'

'Supposing our problem is with the other zones?' asked Simon sullenly. 'When can we start putting that right?'

'We have some rooms, known as AFAs or *Advanced Foreplay Areas*. On your next visit for Session Eight, you will spend the last thirty minutes there.'

'Shall we be alone?'

Donna shook her head. 'There are a few couples who come back to us for refresher courses who are unsupervised in AFA. We call them our trusties. However, for those attending the course for the first time, a counsellor is always on hand to provide advice and guidance.' She smiled as she looked into their anxious faces. 'It can be a little inhibiting at first but couples in therapy soon learn to accept our presence. The counsellor almost becomes another member of the family.'

'That's all very well,' said Simon, 'but when will we be allowed to … do it … properly?'

Donna frowned. 'I'm not sure that I understand you.'

'In your brochure it says that we can have a full and loving union. Isn't that right, Sally?'

'It did say something like that,' said Sally reddening.

'*It said precisely that*,' Simon expostulated, his temper rising.

Donna drew herself up very straight. 'The word "union" is used in the sense of emotional bonding. There is no progression from foreplay to full intimacy. Surely you did not register with the Entente Clinic in the expectation that such a thing would be permitted here?'

'We believed that the Clinic would help us in the area where we were experiencing the greatest difficulty,' Simon grumbled.

'The Clinic can only do so much. Had you attended the Foundation Sessions, I should have felt more confident of the outcome.' With a sharp nod of her head the counsellor went to the door. 'Now, if you will kindly follow me, we shall go to *Activity*.'

Donna led the way to a small room, circular in shape, lit by spotlights recessed into a domed ceiling. On the wall there were pictures illustrating alternative positions of lovemaking. The bodies were almost impossibly brown and beautiful.

'*Activity* practicals take place here,' said Donna. She pointed to the middle of the floor, which was occupied by a large round mattress with a shiny white cover. 'We call this area the Forum.'

'What are those things?' Simon pointed to a strange assortment of objects laid out on a trolley.

'Those are *Activity* aids. You need not concern yourselves with them for the moment.'

Sally gestured in the direction of a curtained archway which led out of the room. 'What happens through there, Donna?'

'There are a number of rooms dedicated to *Advanced Foreplay*.'

'Is there any chance that we–'

'Not today, Sally. When you return here for your final session, you will go to one of our AFAs. Now I want you both to go to the changing cubicles in the corner and remove your clothes. You will find undergarments laid out for you. Please put them on and return here.'

'This is a bit more like it,' Simon murmured as he stripped off. He tapped cheerfully on the partition that separated them.

'What is it?' whispered Sally.

'Things seem to be looking up.'

'What sort of things?' she giggled.

Simon struggled into his underpants. Made of opaque, white elasticised rubber, they reminded him of the surgical gloves that his dentist wore. He gave a little gasp as he saw Sally emerge in a bra and briefs so close fitting that they moulded her body like a second skin.

Donna instructed them to stand facing one another. 'Simon, I want you to take Sally's hands and tell her how much you admire her.'

'Sally, you look pretty good,' said Simon, his cheeks growing hot.

'*Sally, you look pretty good*,' Donna repeated. 'That little speech is what we get from a man who did not attend Session Three and learn about *Language Content*. You must praise her, Simon. Try again.'

Simon lowered his eyes and scuffed his feet on the floor. 'You look beautiful, Sally,' he mumbled.

'Use intensifiers, Simon. You should say, "Sally, you look so beautiful … so desirable…" and you should tell her where she is beautiful and desirable. "Sally, your eyes are marvellous … your body is lovely." Don't drop your eyes, Simon, and stare at her breasts – and don't fidget.'

'I'm sure I shall get better once we make a start,' said Simon.

'I certainly hope so,' replied Donna. She placed a hand on Sally's arm. 'Sally, dear, I want you to take up position on the Forum. Lie down on your front and try to relax.' She took a bottle from the trolley. 'Simon, I am going to put a little lemon balm on the tips of your fingers. For your first *Sensate* exercise, I want you to kneel down beside Sally and apply the balm to the response points on her feet.'

Simon knelt down and stared at Sally's feet in some perplexity. He gripped her right foot by the ankle, lifted it and dabbed at the heel. He turned reproachful eyes on the counsellor. 'Nothing seems to be happening,' he complained. Bereft of inspiration, he scraped a finger along the line of Sally's toes as if they were piano keys.

Sally uttered a cry of discomfort. The soles of her feet curled up like a hedgehog rudely disturbed from a winter's hibernation.

'*No, no, Simon!*' exclaimed Donna. 'Sally found that *most* disagreeable. Let me show you. I am going to put a little oil of sandalwood on my fingers.' She took Simon's place on the mattress and adopted a sitting position. Very gently she lifted the girl's leg and laid it across her lap. 'I am working my fingers over the arch of the foot ... using smooth ... scooping … gliding ... movements … watch how my middle finger slides over the ball of the foot to the toes … nudging between them … separating them ... singling out the little toe for especial homage ... taking it between my finger and thumb ... drawing it up so it stands proud of its companions… … anointing it with aromatic oil ... there, see how it sparkles ... like a small ruby…' Donna exhaled a long, shuddering sigh. She dropped the foot in her lap and leaned back, gripping the edge of the mattress for support. For a moment she seemed too overcome to continue.

Simon bent down. 'Donna, may I have a go?' he pleaded.

Donna rallied herself. 'Have a go? *What an irresistible proposal!* A woman's body is a wonderfully subtle and complex system. Not a coconut shy at a fairground. Watch *carefully*, Simon, and learn.' She placed a little more oil on her fingers. 'For the tight little crease behind the knee I favour oil of juniper. See how I place the calf and upper leg under tension so that the skin is drawn tight over the tissue. Now watch my fingertips, Simon – watch their rhythm, the slow tapotement at first and then building up to a crescendo.' A tremor ran through Sally's body. Her buttocks clenched and then relaxed.

The palms of Simon's hands were damp with perspiration. The blood seemed to be rushing through him like a fleet of express trains all heading for the same terminus. He fiddled feverishly with the pink dots in his envelope. 'Please, Donna, may I place some of the dots on Sally?'

'Not yet, Simon!' There was a note of hysteria in Donna's voice. 'If you had an *ounce* of feeling, you would realise that therapy must *never* be interrupted. Try to show a *little* more consideration.'

'I'm very sorry, Donna—'

'We shall say no more about it. Now I am going to ask Sally to turn over and then we are going to place a pillow under her to release the lower back.' She reached for a pillow. 'Raise yourself, Sally. That's good. Lie back again. Spread your legs a little.' Donna pointed to an implement on the trolley. 'Simon, please pass me the zephyr.'

'The thing with the feathers on it?'

'Yes. Be very careful how you handle it.'

The implement that Donna held in her hands was like a battery-operated hair dryer save for the nozzle, which was encircled with a diadem of white goose feathers. As she pressed a button, a low hum came from the equipment. The feathers quivered, each silky filament stiffening in the air stream.

'Watch carefully, Simon. I am going to work the zephyr up and down the inside of Sally's thighs.' She knelt between Sally's feet and bent forward. 'You will see that I use gentle, rippling movements … the very lightest of touches … combining the warm air current with the tips of the feathers … stimulating the nerve ends … creating wavelets of sensation…'

'May I—?'

'Don't talk, Simon! *Observe!* Notice the slight change in Sally's breathing … how the side walls of her nostrils are widening … how her eyes start to glisten … the pupils to dilate … lines of tension appear around the mouth … her arms stretch out … the fingers vibrating like tuning forks … how her lips begin to swell … to redden … to separate … as if her heart was opening…'

Above the hum of the fan motor, little bubbles of sound could be heard. Donna closed her eyes and turned up the air volume. The bubbles rose ever higher as pleasure approached the brim. Donna's hands fluttered like those of a water diviner nearing the source of a hidden spring. Dimly she heard Simon calling to her. Her hips twitched like the hindquarters of a horse ridding itself of a tiresome insect. *'Be quiet, Simon! Can't you see that I'm trying to concentrate?'*

Donna's excitement mounted as she strained her ears to catch the responses above the whirring of the machine. Simon had gripped her arm. He was shouting. There was no need to shout. If he would only be silent for a few more moments … that was all she asked … a few more moments and then he could make a start with his little pink dots. She shook him off.

'Donna!' Simon yelled.

'Leave me alone, Simon!' Her cheeks were livid patches of red and white as if she had fallen headlong into a nettle bed.

'Donna! Those noises – there are people in the next room!'

'Don't worry about them,' Donna cried. 'It is only Rod and Pam Plonken.'

'But Donna … they are making love!'

'*They are not making love,*' she shrilled. 'They are in *Advanced Foreplay.*' Her voice spiralled ever higher like a whirlwind. 'We encourage couples to articulate pleasurable feelings provided that enthusiasm is kept within bounds.'

'Donna! *Listen!*'

From behind the red curtain that screened the archway leading from the room came wild cries accompanied by the sound of creaking wood and grating metal like an inn sign swinging in a gale.

Donna's mouth opened and closed noiselessly. Her eyes rolled up into her head as if anxious to defer to other senses the unpalatable task of interpretation. Casting the zephyr to one side she rose unsteadily to her feet. 'Sally and Simon …' her voice quavered, 'there may have been a … a serious breach of trust. I must call the Principal to AFA at once. Simon, while I am away, start placing your little pink dots. Begin with Sally's feet.' She ran a distracted hand through her hair and hurried across the room.

'Simon,' Sally whispered.

'Yes, darling.' He knelt down and kissed her eyes shut. Then he removed her bra, tugged down her rubber briefs and then his own.

'What are the Bonkins doing?' she asked softly.

'Each other, it seems. Anyway, the name is Plonken.'

Sally placed her arms about him, pulling him down to her in a long, fluent glide. 'Today is the day that we skate down the rainbow…' she murmured.

'The day … we climb … the Magic Mountain.' His heart seemed to miss a beat as he adjusted himself to the rocking movements of her body.

Dimly, in some part of their consciousness, they were aware of a distant clamour, the echoes and reverberations of pain and discord, but delight was fast overwhelming their senses.

'Take me … higher … Simon, darling … I want … to touch the stars…'

'I want to stand … on top … of the world…'

At that moment Donna pulled back the curtain. Her mouth gaped. The universe did not hold enough air to fill her lungs for the scream that propelled her across the room. Her arms performed a demented semaphore over the lovers. *'Simon!'* she shrieked. 'What *do* you think *you are doing! Stop it! Leave off at once!'* She hopped up and down in a frenzy but the rhythm of the intertwined bodies seemed only to quicken in time with the impromptu accompaniment.

Donna gave a great sob. She turned and fled, running blindly from room to room until she came to *Information and Communication*, where she flung her arms about the latex Venus and buried her burning cheeks among the cool contours of that inviolable bosom. And there she wept.

THE LEARNING CURVE

On Saturday morning, Katie Colville went to the picture framers. She had bought a print as a wedding present for Henry, a view of meadows running down to the cliffs, a walk they had often taken together. A customer was leaving and the door was slightly ajar as she went in.

The shop was divided by a light partition. Beyond it, where the frames were made, she could hear two men talking. Then she realised that there was a bell on top of the door which hadn't rung. They didn't know that she was there.

She had only to close the door, but as she stretched out her arm, she heard the name Lorna Baillie. It made her catch her breath and guiltily she listened.

'I would give anything to see Sir Henry's face when he opens the parcel. He will probably pass out.'

'If he hasn't taken Lorna out of her wrapping by now, he must be a very slow operator. Those two have been engaged for at least a month.'

The other man sighed. 'What it is to be young. When I was your age, a kiss and a cuddle in the back row of the cinema was all that a lad like me could hope for. Even after I had put a wedding ring on the lady's finger, I might have been breaking into the Bank of England from the fuss she made.'

'Did you see that picture of Rawnsley in the *Express*?'

'Standing in front of that great big stone pile? Yes. He looked the genuine article right enough. Tweed jacket, cavalry twills. Labrador in attendance. I bet the dog sleeps on his bed – but not for much longer, if you ask me. Miss Baillie will soon be the one wearing the trousers and Fido will have to doss down in the stables.' There was a rustle of paper.

'*Lorna Baillie!*' His companion whistled softly. 'Wearing nothing but a great big smile.'

'Almost nothing. Look at the wedding veil. Finest Brussels lace. And the bouquet of white lilies. She looks as if she has walked down the aisle strewing her wedding clothes all the way to the altar. You have got to admit that the man has class.'

'It's a great shot.'

'And a lot more fun than his usual stuff.'

'Meaning?'

'He's a children's photographer. Goes to the smart houses. Portrait studies of the spoiled brats squirming in their white ankle socks and patent-leather shoes. Nanny frowning heavily from the doorway. Mummy cooing just off camera. The mums used to be all over him.'

'*Literally?*'

'As match-makers, I trust, but I wouldn't put it past him. Gerald is heir to a peerage. For almost ten years he was one of the country's most eligible bachelors.'

'And now?'

'That label has lost its shine. When his cousin dies, he will come into the title but the rumour is that there isn't much money. The old boy borrowed heavily and you can't spend it more than once.'

'I know you two are old pals but there are limits. Why did he send you the photograph? If he wanted a frame, he could have given you the measurements.'

'I don't know. Spite, maybe. Gerald had a big walk-out with Lorna. She dumped him after a year and that didn't suit. He likes to do the dumping.'

'How did he get her to pose?'

'Who knows? A beautiful woman doesn't mind showing off her body if she gets the right sort of invitation. Gerald told me that he has a safe full of nude photographs – all the girls he has slept with.'

'He sounds a bit kinky.'

'Perhaps he is. He goes for the young ones … two years out of school … a bit lost in the big city … takes them out to dinner, chats them up, and then it's back to his pad … puts on a tape ... smoochy music … low lighting…'

'What's so special about that? It sounds like the old routine.'

'Hang on a moment. Ask yourself how he actually gets these little chicks into bed? For years they have heard Mum and Dad droning on about not getting into trouble and how to defend themselves against the wiles of practised seducers like Gerald Vyse. This is the crisis they have been preparing for ever since they bought their first pair of nylons.'

'So?'

'They dance for a bit. Then move to the sofa…'

'Standard ploy so far.'

'The girl puffing nervously on a cigarette … bracing herself to fend him off … preparing some little speech about getting to know him better before … before becoming too involved…'

'Well, don't just stand there grinning. What happens next? Are you going to tell me or not?'

'It sounds so simple but I wonder how many men would have the balls to do it.'

'Come off it, Malcolm. Stop farting around. *What does he do?*'

'He yawns. Chucks his coat over a chair. Throws his tie after it. Starts to undo the buttons on his shirt. "I'm going to bed," he says. "Are you coming? If not – see yourself out. Go back to Mummy."'

'And pisses off?'

'Yes. The message is get laid – or get lost.'

'Brutal but–'

'Effective – or so he told me.'

'I still think it is a shit's trick for Gerald to send that photograph to Rawnsley. After all, he had his chance with Lorna. Why didn't he marry her himself?'

'One woman could never keep him happy. That's what he told me. He has to play the field. There's always some little innocent who is starting out on the learning curve.'

'I wouldn't mind learning her curves.'

'Dream on. Now, Geoff, I have probably said more than I should. I don't want any gossip over this job. Gerald has given us a lot of business over the years and just for once he doesn't owe us any money. So keep that big mouth of yours buttoned up.'

'You know I don't blab, Malcolm. What Gerald does with his private life is none of my business.'

'That's right. And not so much of the Gerald, if you don't mind. To you he is *Mister* Vyse. To the postman who delivers his mail, he is *The Honourable Gerald Vyse*. To us, he's a valued customer. Got it? Good. Now, I can't stand around chatting all day. I must deliver that frame no later than Monday morning, so don't let me down. *My God! Is it midday already?* I must get back!'

Katie fled the shop. In the street she wondered why people were staring at her and then she found that she was running. What a sight she must look with her hair all awry, her cheeks burning, the wind flicking away the tears from the corners of her eyes. *Poor, darling Henry!* Was it possible that such gratuitous, senseless cruelty existed? And that it should be visited on him, of all people?

She had been in love with Henry since she was eight. They had met at a children's party. Playing sardines. Or was it murder? And he had held her hand when they hid in that huge, dark wardrobe at the end of the gallery and told her not to be frightened for he would protect her. After all, he said, he was two years older than she. And when you are eight, two years is an eternity. Henry was all the knights in shining armour rolled into one.

Katie shared a flat in London but home to her was the long, low-built stone building that had once been two workmen's cottages and where her parents lived a cramped but cheerful existence. Her father was manager of a large farm close to the Rawnsley estate. From her bedroom window she could see the top of the chimneys of Trystan Hall, the draughty, rambling old house where, after his parents died, Henry lived with only his housekeeper and his dog for company.

Henry was an only child and Katie's sister was a lot older, so they had been much thrown together. Her mother said that they were just like brother and sister. Her mother had a horror of 'complications' arising from her daughter's friendship, complications which might, she feared, give rise to the suspicion that her family was taking advantage of the fact that the Rawnsleys were neighbours. It made Katie's blood boil.

As she reached the river, she slowed to a walk, stopping for a moment on Battersea Bridge to catch her breath before turning into the park. It was a raw April afternoon, the clouds scudding before a stiff breeze and the light branches of the trees beating up and down as if to keep themselves warm.

Katie usually lingered at the adventure playground to look at the children but today she passed them without a second glance, skirting the miniature lakes, listening to the soles of her shoes on the tarmac paths as if they could tap out some message of warning to Henry over the scores of miles that separated them.

She could see Henry now, striding across those undulating fields bounded by the bleak dry-stone walls, the dog loping along at his heels. He would be hatless, his dark hair a little too long, almost covering his ears, his coat collar turned up against the knifing wind off the sea.

Henry had wanted to stay in the army but his father had died very suddenly and then his mother within the year. The estate was losing a lot of money and he had to learn fast if he was going to turn things around. Then he had been offered a good price by a company that wanted the land for clay or aggregates or something. Nine out of ten people in his position would have taken the money and sold up, but Henry had not been sure that the farm workers and their families would have been looked after. He had turned it down.

'I wouldn't have had two pennies worth of enjoyment knowing that they might lose their jobs and their cottages.' Henry had shrugged in that self-deprecating way he had. 'I know it's fossilised to think like that these days but it's the only drill I know.'

His engagement to Lorna Baillie was the last thing Katie had been expecting. Henry telephoned to tell her. 'It has all happened so quickly, Katie, but I had to tell you first. You must meet Lorna. She is a feature writer and apparently quite well known. I have never met anyone like her. She throws off sparks like a Catherine wheel. What she sees in me I can't imagine…'

She had let him carry on while she tried to rally herself. She was being childish. Henry owed her nothing. Weren't they just friends? So why did she feel like a small boat that had been knocked over by a giant wave?

But he spoke quickly, defensively, as if he was piling up a wall of sandbags between them, as if he feared she might overwhelm him with a flood of reproaches before he had finished. 'I know twenty-two is young to be getting married but farming can be a lonely business and I have a dread of becoming fusty and set in my ways.'

'You could never become fusty, Henry,' she had protested.

'I'm not so sure. Anyway, there's no chance of that with Lorna about the place. She will blow the cobwebs away.'

Her heart had cried out at the injustice of it. She might not have Lorna Baillie's looks or sophistication but what were those compared with the love, the loyalty, the devotion that she could give him? But her heart, she told herself, was a fool. Henry might care for her a little but why should he marry her? He had found this exciting, exotic creature who would make him happy. That was what mattered. 'I'm delighted for you, Henry. When is the–?'

'Early in June. Lorna insists on a large wedding. She has found a church in Eaton Square which holds a multitude. I wanted something simpler, more private … but I mustn't be selfish. She has loads of friends and she wants them all to come. You must support the home team, Katie. I fear we shall be heavily outnumbered.'

In her mind she could see Henry at that reception, doing the rounds of the guests. Fretting in his stiff collar like a badly bridled horse, stooping a little to catch the sense of what was being said to him, the shy smile emerging from that self-communing absorption, the glimmer of deliverance in his eye as he caught sight of the estate workers and their families in their garrison around the tea urn, Lorna frothing lace like an iced-over fountain, fixing him with a cold eye, leading him away with whispered reminders of his duties.

'Early June? As soon as that?' Six weeks. *Six short weeks*.

'Yes. Lorna doesn't believe in long engagements. And, of course, we must be back home in July for the harvest.'

Lorna Baillie. Katie had recognised the name. She was always in the weekend colour supplements with her articles on dining out or travel or some other aspect of the glitzy world she moved in. In the glossy magazines there were often pictures of her at race meetings, fashion shows, charity dances, film premieres and so on. She had an air of controlled energy. Striking looks. Fair hair cut close to the head, wide-set blue eyes and a brilliant smile. She had a slim, boyish figure, lovely long legs.

Katie sat on a bench looking out over the sluggish brown river. What was she to do? Should she try to warn Lorna? She shrank from the very idea. Lorna and she lived in different worlds. They should have met at the engagement party but Katie had a frightful cold and had missed it. She had felt like a coward and a traitor but she couldn't appear with her streaming eyes and scarlet nose, couldn't face her rival's disdainful sympathy as Henry introduced them.

A friend who had gone to the party telephoned her. 'What a pity you weren't there, Katie. Lorna is a revelation, so stylish and amusing. I have never seen Henry so fired up. He is obviously completely smitten.'

'How old do you think she is?' The question sounded so crude that she was ashamed of having uttered it.

'Three or four years older than us. About twenty-four I would guess. Of course, she has been around a bit.'

'What do you mean by that?' Katie pursued, hating herself for her disloyalty to Henry, for the pleasure it would give her to discover that Lorna was something short of perfection.

'Lorna has had one or two quite serious affairs but she has been very discreet. She never got talked about.'

'Do you think she is right for Henry? I just can't see a woman like that settling at Trystan.'

'Tripping out in her Ferragamo shoes to feed the pigs. Is that what you mean?'

'You know I don't mean that. Henry has plenty of help on the place. But Lorna isn't bred to the life. After the first few months, when the excitement has worn off … when she is moving buckets in the passage because the rain is coming through the roof…'

'I think you underestimate Lorna. We couldn't do her job but–'

'She could do ours,' Katie sighed heavily. She found a straw and clutched at it. 'What about Lorna's career? Can you see her throwing up all that to live at Trystan? Wouldn't she miss the big city, the buzz, the pressure?'

'And the rest of the social merry-go-round? I don't know. Perhaps she is tired of all that. Maybe she wants to settle down and start a family.'

'Do you think that someone like Lorna, a woman with so many claims on her time and on her talents, can really fall in love?'

Her friend had laughed. 'You want me to say that only susceptible idiots like you and I can lose our hearts. But isn't that rather arrogant?'

'I suppose it is…'

'I don't think you need worry too much about Henry. Lorna will pull her weight. She will have amusing, interesting people to the house. You must admit that Henry needs digging out of his rut. He has lived like a monk for too long. There is a rather solitary side to him. He was an only child, of course.'

Katie walked slowly back to her flat still carrying the unframed print. The picture seemed irrelevant now. By Tuesday morning, Henry would have that ghastly photograph. The engagement would be broken off. He would take it very hard. Retreat into his shell like a hermit crab, never to re-emerge. And she would be to blame. She should have done something.

That night she didn't sleep a wink. The night following, exhausted, she finally slept but awoke at five. Two hours later she was opening up the small children's clothes shop in Fulham where she worked. At eight, she telephoned Amanda Rowse at home. Amanda would know about Gerald Vyse. Amanda knew everything. Katie said a silent prayer that Algy had left for the City and they could talk freely.

Amanda giggled. 'I am all alone with Tom. He's having his breakfast. A double milk shake.'

'Lucky Tom.'

'Isn't he? But I know you didn't telephone to talk about him. Not at this time of day. It must be love trouble.'

'*It's not love trouble,*' replied Katie indignantly. 'It's about a man called Vyse.'

'*Gerald Vyse?* Then it's the worst sort of love trouble.'

'I have never set eyes on him, Amanda. I just want–'

'To know about him.' She giggled again. 'He must be almost forty … and he is hardly your type.'

'There's this friend of mine who wants to–'

'*Oh, come off it, Katie!* Don't play that corny old tune. You want to meet Gerald. And why shouldn't you? He split up with Lorna Baillie a couple of months ago. The word on the street is that she gave him the chop and that he's still licking his wounds. So you can catch him on the rebound. Perfect timing!'

'For heaven's sake! *I don't want to catch him!* All I am trying to do is–'

'Broaden your education. And what better way than with an experienced older man.'

'*Amanda!* You are quite impossible!'

'*Nonsense*! I just call a spade a spade. And I call Gerald Vyse a wolf. Let's start with his lair. He lives in a charming flat in Chelsea.' She mentioned a garden square close to the Kings Road. 'He is heir to a peerage. The title comes to him when his cousin dies. So when you are lying in Gerald's arms–'

'I don't intend to lie in his arms, Amanda.'

'Then you must see something in Gerald that I have missed. And it can't be money. Most of the tradesmen in London have knocked on his door at one time or another trying to get their bills paid.'

'What has he been doing all these years? He doesn't sound like a businessman.'

'He was in Naval Intelligence until about five years ago. He still is but it's spelled differently. Don't waste time asking about that part of his life. You won't learn anything.'

'And now he's a professional photographer?'

'He would hate to be called a professional. He tells everyone that he does it for fun.'

'But presumably he needs the money?'

'Yes. And I believe he is quite good. He gets on with young children. You know how difficult they can be. The little girls pulling their skirts over their heads, the boys tearing around showing off.'

'How does he spend his day? Has he a routine?'

'Gerald is the most predictable man that I know. He gets up at a quarter to eight and opens the curtains. After that, he does fifteen minutes yoga. Then he puts on a silk dressing gown and makes breakfast – usually for two. Grapefruit, hot croissants, marmalade or honey and fresh-ground coffee.'

'How do you know all this, Amanda?'

'How do you think? Now, don't interrupt. Where were we?'

'Having breakfast after a steamy night.'

'So we were. In the summer, he moves the breakfast table out onto the balcony which makes all his neighbours late for work.'

'Peering through their curtains to see–'

'Who the dolly bird is this time. By nine o'clock he has waved her into a taxi. He reads the paper for half an hour then his valet arrives and runs a bath for him and sorts out his clothes. There is a daily woman who cleans the flat, hand-launders his shirts and does the shopping.

'Between ten and twelve he goes into purdah. He shuts himself in his darkroom developing and printing his photographs. At midday he emerges, makes a few telephone calls, writes the odd letter before changing for lunch. He is out between two and four in the afternoon seeing clients.'

'Where does he go for lunch?'

'He always goes to Sam's. Gets there on the dot of one.'

'Where is Sam's?'

'*Don't you know Sam's?* Katie, where have you been all your life? It's a bar just off St James's Square.'

'Surely I can't go there by myself?'

'You can say you are waiting for a friend. Look at your watch every few minutes. Then frown and glance at the door. That's what I did. I went there sometimes if I was between men or feeling a bit down.'

Katie had scribbled some notes. She thanked Amanda.

'One other thing…'

'Yes?'

'If you see Gerald in the evening, don't wear tights. He hates them. Wear stockings and choose a good brand. And don't go back to his flat unless you want the whole performance. He has a large double bed and makes very imaginative use of it. And good luck.' Amanda was still giggling when she rang off.

At a quarter to one, Katie changed in the back of the shop. The pit of her stomach seemed to be going up and down like the floor of a high-speed elevator. She must be crazy to think that she could outwit a man like Gerald Vyse. Wouldn't she do better to throw herself on his mercy? Beg him not to send that photograph? But he would just laugh in her face.

The lemon-yellow coat and skirt had looked great on her the previous evening as she rehearsed in front of the mirror. Now, on a dull grey afternoon, she looked like a moulting canary. She locked up, hoping that Mrs Willoughby wouldn't catch her sneaking out early. Her employer came in afternoons to help out, rarely omitting to help herself from the cash till at the same time.

A taxi took her to the top of Jermyn Street. She decided to walk the last fifty yards. The skirt was cut rather high. It was tight around her hips. She must look like a streetwalker down on her luck. Well, what if she did. *Fight fire with fire*! She unfastened the button of her jacket, allowing her blouse to fill out a little.

Sam's was tucked away in a tiny cobbled courtyard that she had not known existed. It was the clubby sort of place that a man like Gerald Vyse would have used. On the walls there were prints of old cars, a moth-eaten woodcock in a glass case, a fading photograph of a polo game at Hurlingham, leather-bound books in alcoves either side of the fireplace.

A few men in business suits were drinking shorts but they were outnumbered by the blazer brigade who held beer tankards in their hands. An attractive girl with a valiant smile was pretending to listen to a story about a man who had scored in the car park at Twickenham at half time.

'They should have saved him one of the oranges,' someone chortled.

Under cover of the laughter, Katie took a high stool at the bar and ordered a rum and Coca-Cola, a drink she had never had in her life. Sam, the bartender, reached for a glass above his head. He was overweight and the immaculate white linen jacket two sizes too small for him.

'Ice and lemon?'

Katie nodded.

Sam cut a slice of lemon and dropped it in the glass. 'I don't remember seeing you here before.'

'I haven't been here for some time,' Katie lied. Following Amanda's precepts, she glanced down at her watch and then at the door. She wondered if her cheeks looked as hot as they felt.

One of the men left the group and there was a momentary lull in the conversation as heads turned to follow him. Mindful that it might be poor tactics to turn his way, Katie buried her nose in her glass.

'Get on with dispensing your poison, Sam, and stop bullying the customers,' the newcomer said. He leaned over the bar and adjusted the barman's red bow tie. 'Your starboard wing has dropped, Sam. Try to come to work properly dressed in future.'

'I will do my best, Mr Vyse,' replied Sam imperturbably and went on polishing the already gleaming glasses.

'Can you put your hand on a bottle of Bolly, Sam?'

'Of course, Sir.'

'Then cut a hole in the ice and pull it out.'

'Coming up now, Mr Vyse.' There was a pop as he extracted the cork and poured the foaming liquid into a single flute.

'Another glass, Sam, please. You know I hate drinking by myself.' He turned to Katie and pointed at the stool on which her hand was resting. 'I was rather hoping that you were keeping that for me.'

'I was expecting someone … to … to join me,' Katie stammered, thrown into confusion by the dark, challenging eyes fixed on her.

'That someone has arrived – and with a bottle of champagne.'

'What about your friends?' Her large grey eyes turned anxiously to the group that her new companion had deserted.

Vyse put his mouth close to her ear. 'I'm bored with them. They talk about nothing but racing or polo or sailing and I wanted to talk about you instead.' He folded her fingers gently in his before releasing them with some reluctance and introducing himself. 'You must stay for a bite of lunch. Sam has a wonderful way with a prawn.' He swung up onto the stool next to her.

In a sort of daze, Katie heard herself mumbling her name and watching the champagne turn from white to gold in her glass. Her fingers were still tingling where he had touched them. The contact seemed to drive every coherent thought from her head. An hour later she was struggling to remember anything that he had said. She tried to recall his features. Black hair brushed back from the forehead, dark eyes set wide apart, a lopsided smile which softened the cruel mouth, strong white teeth contrasting with the heavy suntan. She could recall nothing more, except that the prawn salad was superb, the Brie exquisite and she had agreed to have dinner with him that evening.

She wasn't more than a few minutes late getting back to work but she must have seemed flustered for she received a curious look from Mrs Willoughby.

'Are you quite sure that you are alright, Katie dear? You look as if you might be running a slight temperature.'

'Quite sure, Mrs Willoughby, thank you,' she replied firmly. But she made two mistakes with prices within the hour, driving her close to despair. What hope had she of rescuing Henry if she couldn't do better than this? Far from being in charge of events, she was barely mistress of herself. By now Gerald Vyse would have that appalling photograph. What if he had already posted it? Her campaign would be in ruins. She would have lost before she started.

Vyse had wanted to collect her from her flat in Battersea but Katie made the excuse that she had been invited for a drink with friends in Chelsea. The less he knew about her the better. They agreed to meet outside the cinema opposite the old Town Hall. She almost forgot Amanda's warning about tights being taboo. After work she just managed to get to the shops before they closed. Buying the stockings gave her a strange sensation. It was like going into an angling shop for a pound of live bait. This time she was the bait.

Mercifully, Susie, her flatmate, had gone to a drinks party and wasn't there to watch her dress. To see her sheathe her slim legs in the sheer nylon stockings. To help her button herself into the blue satin dress. To interrogate her. Who's the new man, Katie? Do I know him? Where did you find him? Where are you going? Oh, Katie, don't be mean. *Do tell!*

She was giving the tilted tip of her nose a final dust in front of the mirror when a small jar of pills on the glass shelf over the basin caught her eye. Susie's sleeping tablets! Available on prescription only. And very strong. She put two of them into a tissue and pushed them down the front of her dress. Susie would never miss them.

Katie gave herself a final inspection in the full-length mirror. She pinched her cheeks to bring some colour to them. She felt a little faint. The moment had come. What was her plan? Her strategy? She had none. She must win Vyse's confidence and watch for an opportunity.

She closed her eyes and muttered a little prayer. Henry's face shimmered into focus … she could see him sitting at the end of the long dining table … turning over that package in his hands … untying the string … undoing the wrapping paper … perhaps wondering if it was a wedding present from her. *It was ghastly!* She pummelled her forehead with her fists to shake the images out of her head. Picking up her coat, she ran down the stairs to the street.

She didn't have to wait. On the dot of nine, Gerald drove up in a sporty black saloon. He was wearing a dark-blue blazer with shiny Service buttons. The cream silk shirt bore his initials over the pocket. In his hand was a bunch of red roses.

'These are for you.'

'You shouldn't have… Oh! They are lovely … what are they called?'

'Escapade.'

'That sounds rather irresponsible.'

'I feel rather irresponsible.' He opened the passenger door. She could feel his eyes appraising her as she joined her knees and swung her legs into the car, the hem of her dress riding an inch or two up her thighs. They drove to a restaurant that she had never been to before. Heads turned as she floated in on his arm.

'Has anyone ever told you that you have got the most wonderful legs?'

'*Gerald*! Everyone in the room must have heard that.'

'What of it? If I admire something, why should I keep quiet about it? As for that long chestnut hair of yours – I imagine waking up in the morning and finding it spread across my pillow.'

'Gerald! *Not so loud!*' She gripped his arm fiercely. 'Do you *always* carry on like this?'

Vyse tapped her fingers with his. 'Invariably.'

Katie let him order for her just as she let him tell her about the miraculous colour of her eyes and the sublime texture of her skin and the sensuous way she moved. For a time she held out, rolling coil after coil of wire between them, but he just snipped his way through them, one after the other.

'And I love the way you laugh – it reminds me of dark-blue hyacinths.'

'I don't believe it. You're teasing me.'

'You must learn to accept a compliment.'

'That takes practice and we poor English girls get so little of it.'

'You don't pamper your men like the Continental women.'

'The Continental men cherish their women.'

'So do I.'

'You make it sound as if you keep a harem in the spare bedroom.'

He laughed, his hands coming gently together as if already closing about her waist. Two hours had flown as if she had been in a trance. Everything was in soft focus, the pale-pink tablecloths, the roses in the vase between them, the low murmur of conversation.

Katie sipped from the glass in her hand. The light from the candle turned the wine to a warm red glow. 'I am puzzled that a man who has a certain maturity–'

'Maturity! Oh Lord! *Spare us!*' Vyse groaned.

'I don't think of you as old … seasoned, perhaps … is that so terrible?'

'Go on. Now say something nice.'

'Why should a man who is good-looking,' she persisted, 'charming … accomplished … who has had a certain experience of women …'

'Be attracted by a beautiful young woman? And want to possess her? Is that so very strange?'

'But is it a fair contest?'

'Why should I want that? A good general will always look for an advantage … ground of his choosing … superior forces … the element of surprise.'

'It sounds most unsporting.'

'It is. There is very little that is sporting about raising one's gun and bringing down a nice hen pheasant. But I do it and enjoy it.'

'If you had to spend your next existence as an animal and could choose the species, what would you be?'

'A lion.'

Katie reflected for a moment. 'A lion stalking a herd of gazelle will pick out one fully grown, one that will make a good meal – unless his…' she hesitated.

'Unless the old boy's battery is running down. Unless he has lost his speed and strength and must rely on cunning.' He took a silver case from his pocket and flipped the lid open. 'That is what you meant, isn't it?'

She watched him light up before replying. 'I wouldn't have put it so bluntly.'

'But that is how you regard me – middle-aged and predatory?'

Katie smiled. 'And immoral.'

He drew on his cigarette and released a thin spiral of smoke. 'Isn't immorality a rather old-fashioned idea?'

'As old-fashioned as the notion that it is wrong to take something that doesn't belong to you. There was a time when that was called stealing.'

'If I covet something and can persuade the owner to part with it, surely that isn't stealing?'

The lights in the restaurant dimmed. He stubbed out the cigarette. There was silence between them for some moments. 'Dear Katie, so serious-eyed.' He stretched across the table to unravel her fingers and held her hands between his own. 'Tell me. Do you like dancing?'

' I love it.'

'Let's go to my place and put a tape in the machine.'

'Your place?' Her eyebrows went up to register a reservation. She might need it later.

'Yes. Ground of my choosing. Remember, we talked about it a moment ago.'

'Well … I mustn't be late. Before the moon rises this hen pheasant must be up on her branch, safe from poachers and foxes and other predators.'

'You must post your own look-out. The moon and I are barely on nodding terms.' He signed the bill and called for their coats.

As Katie got into the car she caught a glimpse of their waiter in gloomy conference with the restaurant manager. It made her feel ashamed. She would telephone in a week or two. If the money was still owed, she would pay it herself.

Vyse drove well but fast and it was not many minutes before they turned off the road into a leafy square. The car drew up in front of a house looking over a large railed garden. Katie stepped into a pool of amber light thrown by a tall lamp-post. A faint perfume of lilac was borne on the night air.

'Welcome to Bluebeard's castle,' Vyse whispered. He opened the door and his fingers kept a gentle pressure in the small of her back as they climbed a flight of stairs to the first floor. On either side there were sporting prints, scenes of India under the British Raj; cavalrymen in splendid uniforms with lances lowered, galloping after wild pigs; fierce-looking men in khaki sun helmets mounted on elephants, firing rifles

at tigers. The pigs and the tigers seemed to be having
the worst of the sport.

Vyse opened another door and led the way into a
hall. In the corner stood a long-case clock. There was a
post table to which her eyes darted but it was bare save
for a pair of antique duelling pistols. They walked past
a rack with coats and capes, a stand with walking sticks,
regimental photographs, an old barometer.

He took her coat and ushered her into the sitting
room.

'Low lighting, soft music?'

'Naturally. I am hoping you will prove
susceptible.' He turned on a table lamp and threw a log
into the hearth, sending sparks like fireflies up the
chimney.

Katie's eyes travelled slowly around the room.
Family portraits hung from the walls. The shelves of a
tall, narrow bookcase were stocked with thrillers and
military memoirs. A writing desk with a burgundy
leather top was furnished with Victorian inkwells in
glass and silver, an ivory paper knife and photographs
in silver frames. In front of the window was a round
dining table.

There were two other doors. Both closed. One must
lead to the kitchen, the other to the bedroom. She was
intrigued by a crimson curtain on a long wooden pole
which took up one half of a wall. What went on behind
that curtain?

Vyse kissed her lightly on the lips. 'A glass of
peach brandy?'

'A small glass–'

'As small as you like.' He pointed to a bottle and two handsome balloon glasses on the drinks tray. 'Be a darling and do the honours while I put on some music.'

Out of the corner of her eye, she could see him shuffling through some cassettes. This was her chance. Feverishly she reached inside her dress, pulled out the pills wrapped in their tissue, ground them between her finger and thumb to a fine powder and dropped them into his glass. She swirled the brandy around until all traces of the powder had disappeared.

He raised his glass to her and drank. He frowned. 'It's sharper than I remember … not so round, not so smooth…' his arm encircled her waist, 'but Katie, you are round and smooth and perfectly delicious. So who cares?' Deftly, he removed her glass and in a fluent gliding movement led her into a dance.

'You dance beautifully,' he murmured, running his fingers down her neck, steadying her as she stiffened, lightly tracing the lines of her body, coaxing from her a suppleness, a yielding to the swaying rhythm and the dreamy notes of the saxophone.

She must not weaken, she told herself. She must be resolute. She tried to summon a harrowing picture of Henry but the image was too hazy to fortify her. She pointed to the recessed area concealed from her. 'Gerald, tell me, what do you keep hidden behind that mysterious curtain?'

'My trophies,' Vyse whispered in her ear. 'The heads of all the beautiful damsels that I have enticed to my hunting lodge and ravished.' He manoeuvred her to the side of the room and drew aside the curtain to reveal three shallow steps leading up to a platform. 'That is my studio.'

Katie gazed at the large white screen at the back of the recess, her eyes moving to the lights on their metal stilts and the tripod in the foreground. A door in the wall bore a notice marked *Darkroom. Keep Out!*

'What is the screen for?' she asked.

'Behind the screen is a projector. I have only to select a slide to have a background for my portraits.' He held her at arms' length and examined her with what might have passed for a professional eye but for the mobile mouth which hinted at different and hitherto unrealised ambitions. 'Where do you see yourself, Katie? A canal side in Venice? A riverboat in Paris? A fountain in Rome?'

'They sound much too grand for a peasant like me.'

He pursed his lips. 'With that peachy complexion of yours, maybe the countryside would suit you better. A pastoral idyll, perhaps.'

'Marie Antoinette on a milking stool?'

'Much too dressy.'

'A shepherdess? With a fierce collie to protect me.'

'You would make a lovely shepherdess. A pretty straw hat with a blue silk ribbon for your head, a crook in your hand.'

'With a matching bow halfway up the handle.'

'You've got the idea.' He stepped up to the platform and moved the arc lights into position.

'You aren't seriously thinking of taking my photograph?'

'Certainly I am going to take your photograph. I will make you look wonderful.'

Humour him a little, she told herself. But keep him under control. She ran her hands down the front of her dress. 'A satin dress doesn't sound very practical for the fells and the dales.'

He busied himself with the tripod. 'Don't worry about the dress. You won't be wearing one.'

For a moment Katie was struck dumb. She advanced to the foot of the steps, clasped her hands in front of her and took a deep breath. 'If you think that I'm going to prance around in my underclothes–'

'I don't. We decided on the hat. That is all you will be wearing.'

'If that is your idea of a joke…'

'I never joke about my work.'

She put a foot on the first step. 'Gerald, this has been a lovely evening so far but if you are going to spoil it, I'm going back to my flat.'

'You aren't going anywhere. Not until you have paid your debts.' He came to the edge of the platform, folded his arms and looked down at her from his vantage point.

Katie felt the blood drain from her face. She stared at the impassive figure above her like a child looking up at a statue. 'My debts? I don't understand.'

He shrugged. 'It is very simple. The game is over. You have gambled and lost. It is time to pay up.'

The blood ebbed back into her face. She could feel the colour mounting to her cheeks like a crimson tide. 'What do you mean?'

'You have been deceitful. Worse still, you have been found out.'

'How have I deceived you?' She couldn't meet his eyes. Guilt must be written all over her face.

'You're not the sort of girl who hangs out at Sam's hoping for a free meal. You were–'

'I was waiting for a friend.'

'I don't believe that story. Someone told you that I go to Sam's at lunchtime every day. You went there with the intention of meeting me.'

'You introduced yourself.'

'You baited the trap. I walked into it.'

Katie swallowed hard, squared her shoulders, trying to rally herself. 'If you think that I went to Sam's with the sole object of making my number with you! *Why! Of all the conceited–*'

'Bluster won't get you anywhere. I did some checking on you this afternoon. Your home is in Cornwall and within a mile of Trystan Hall, the family seat of a certain Henry Rawnsley, Baronet. Rawnsley is engaged to a friend of mine. Someone I was very close to until recently.'

'So what? Henry and I are old friends. We grew up together. It is no more than coincidence.'

'I don't believe in coincidences.' He went to the telephone and dialled a number.

Her heart was pounding. Surely he couldn't be ringing the police? She knew nothing about the law. Was what she had done criminal?'Gerald, I admit that-'

'Save your breath. I don't need to be told what I know already.' She listened, dry mouthed. He spoke to an all-night courier service. He had a package to be delivered.

'When can you collect it? In an hour? Alright, but don't be later.' He replaced the receiver.

'Please don't send it, Gerald.'

'Send what?'

'That photograph of Lorna.'

'Lorna? Do you know Lorna Baillie?'

'No. But I know that there is a photograph of Lorna.'

'Lorna is engaged to be married. There are probably lots of photographs of her.' His eyes seemed to drift out of focus as if he was busy calculating the number of times her picture had been taken in recent weeks.

She locked her fingers together, twisting them this way and that. 'You are so cruel, Gerald. You know perfectly well which photograph I mean. I implore you not to send it.'

Vyse ran a hand over his dark jowl. 'Why shouldn't I?'

'It will make Henry absolutely wretched.'

'Have you seen the photograph?'

'No. But–'

'If you haven't seen it, how can–'

'I don't need to see it. I have heard about it.'

Vyse rubbed the back of his neck. He gave an impression of bafflement, of someone trying to catch up with events that had run a little ahead of him. Then he smiled. 'Rawnsley might not see the funny side straight away. He probably wouldn't display it in the drawing room at Trystan. But, in time, wouldn't it grow on him?'

'You know it wouldn't. To have his fiancée flaunting her–'

'Her nakedness at the breakfast table? I suppose it would have the poor fellow choking over his kedgeree.'

'To you it is just a joke.' Katie scuffed her feet miserably. 'But Henry isn't like you. He is the soul of honour.'

'He sounds a frightful bore. Up to his knees in mud most of the time and nothing in his head except the price of cow cake.'

'How can you be so foul?'

'I have nothing against Henry Rawnsley personally except that Lorna is engaged to him.'

'I hope they are very happy. Henry idolises her.'

'Lorna is much too lively to be enshrined as Trystan's household deity. Your friend Henry will soon find that out.' Vyse came down the steps. 'By the way, how did you find out about the photograph?'

Katie stepped back. 'I went into the picture framer and heard those two freaks drooling over it.'

'Malcolm and Geoff. They aren't bad chaps. A bit humourless.'

'There was no shortage of hilarity. How could you do such a thing? It was despicable.'

'It was a bit of fun.'

'It was hateful.'

'We shall never agree. But tell me how you planned to intervene and spare the blushes of the saintly Henry?'

'I had no plan. I thought that if I could get invited back here...' A tear trickled down her cheek. 'Gerald, if you have a spark of decency...'

'It's no good appealing to my better nature. We have already agreed that I haven't one.'

'I will do anything ... almost anything ... if–'

'If I don't send that photograph to Henry?' He rubbed his chin. 'Well, I can see a possible solution.'

'What is that?' Not even a glimmer of hope brightened her eye.

'Let me take that photograph of you?'

'In the nude?'

'Oh, no. I do have some principles. I shall provide you with a hat. One with a nice wide brim.'

'The hat is a great comfort,' she said gloomily.

'Cheer up. You will look a dream.'

'How do you know? You just want me to undress so that you can ogle at me.'

'I want you to undress because you will be even more beautiful without your clothes. I want to capture that beauty.'

'That's what I'm afraid of.'

'Dare a little. You have only one high card. You must play it.'

'If I let you …' she began doubtfully, 'do you promise that Lorna's photo…?'

'That photograph will not go to her betrothed. You have my word.'

'How do I know that the photograph has not already been sent to him?'

'You heard me speak to the courier.'

'I heard you gabble into the phone. That's all.'

'What a suspicious creature you are.' From his pocket he extracted a bunch of keys. 'Come with me, Katie.' He walked to the fireplace, placed one foot on the leather top of the fender, reached up and removed the picture hanging over the mantelpiece to reveal the steel door of a wall safe. He unlocked the safe, swung open the door and indicated a square package. 'The photograph is inside. Now do you believe me?'

'You swear it?'

'As an officer and a gentleman.' He re-locked the safe and glanced at his watch. 'Make up your mind, Katie. The messenger will be here within the hour.'

Katie closed her eyes. She took a deep breath. 'If I do this, do you promise not to bandy my photograph around?'

Vyse grinned, showing his strong white teeth. 'I shall enlarge it and send it to your parents, your employer and the local vicar, in that order.'

'Gerald, do be serious.'

'I am being serious.' He yawned and stretched. 'I shall enclose a note to say that it has been rejected by the *News of the World*, the *Sunday Mirror* and several pin-up magazines but, in the expectation that there may be some sentimental interest–'

'You wouldn't!'

'No! I wouldn't!' He turned her around and ran down the zip fastener on the back of her dress.

'Take your hands off me!' she shouted at him. 'I can manage perfectly well without your help.'

'*Well, manage quicker!* I'm tired.' He loosened his tie, went to the door in the corner, opened it and disappeared. She observed that he had left it ajar and by moving a few steps, she could peep through the doorway. From her new position she could see the foot of a four-poster bed; Gerald's hand reaching for a silk dressing gown; then his blazer, tie, shirt, trousers, socks and underclothing being cast on a chair. Aghast, she cried out, *'Gerald! What are you doing in there!'*

'Getting into something comfortable, you little fool. Those arc lights in the studio are very hot. Now hurry up and let's have no more of your adolescent squawks.'

Katie lifted her dress over her head. 'I hate you, Gerald Vyse. I loathe you. I revile you.' She kicked off her shoes. 'I cannot find words to express the contempt

I feel for you.' Her shift fell in a little pool of silk on the floor. The stockings followed. She tiptoed in her undergarments to the fireplace and sat huddled on the fender, looking into the flames. This couldn't be happening. It was just a bad dream. Any moment she would wake up.

'Don't be such a little prude,' Vyse called out from his bedroom. 'Take everything off.'

In a frenzy of rage she removed her knickers and bra, ran across the room and hurled them through the doorway. *'There! Are you satisfied!'* She hared back, mounted the steps to the raised platform and swathed the curtain about her.

When Gerald returned, he was wearing a turquoise silk dressing gown. In one hand he carried a camera, in the other a hurricane lamp. On his feet was a pair of velvet slippers with a crest monogrammed on the toes.

'Where is my straw hat?' She tightened her grip on the curtain.

'I can't find it. I must have mislaid it. We shall have to improvise.' He turned on two arc lights, moved a reflector screen and mounted the camera on the tripod. 'Come into the middle of the studio.'

Reluctantly, Katie left her sanctuary and stepped tentatively into the centre of the platform.

'There is no need to be shy. You have a marvellous body. Exult in it.'

'I don't know what to do with my hands…'

'Then hold this.' He handed her the lamp. 'You can be one of the foolish virgins from the parable in the Bible. Try to look the part.'

'How? I'm not an actress.'

'You have done very well so far.'

'You will have to remind me ... I have forgotten the story.'

'Did you go to Sunday school?'

'No.'

'You modern girls are all pagans.' He scratched his head.

'You can't remember either,' she said accusingly.

'I remember the bits that matter. It was midnight and there was this wedding. There were ten virgins who took their lamps and went to meet the bridegroom…'

'It sounds a most improper story. Are you sure that it comes from the Bible?'

'Quite sure,' he said bracingly. 'There were five wise virgins and five foolish virgins. The wise virgins arrived with oil for their lamps so they were allowed into the marriage feast. But the foolish virgins were locked out because–'

'They had forgotten their oil,' Katie recited wearily. 'You make it all sound very dull.'

'It's only a small part but you must do your best with it.' He placed the flat of his hand under her chin to raise it. His fingers moved to her arm. 'Not so rigid, Katie. You aren't holding a fish that has been dead for a week. Think of yourself as an exquisite marble by Canova, all gleaming curves and contours.'

'Like this?'

'No.' He moved closer. 'And stop scowling like a bad-tempered schoolmistress.' With a finger he stroked her long, dark eyelashes. 'You have lovely eyes, Katie. Show them off. Look up at the lamp. Try to convey your feelings at this moment. Shock. Dismay. Apprehension.'

'Like this?'

'Not quite. Shape your lips prettily. You look as if your teeth have got wedged on a piece of chewing gum.'

Katie's arm drooped. 'It's hopeless. Why can't I be a wise virgin?'

'Because, I don't think you are a wise virgin.'

'Which do you mean?' Her eyes flashed angrily. 'That I'm a fool or I'm not … not a–'

'Don't ask so many questions. It's getting late.' He selected a slide from a box against the skirting. 'Watch the screen behind you. I'm going to switch on the projector.'

A village street appeared on the screen. A man leading a donkey laden with panniers was making his way up a hill between whitewashed houses. The setting sun cast dramatic shadows.

'It doesn't look a bit like the Holy Land. It's more like Majorca.'

'It is Majorca. But it will have to do.'

'Where is the marriage feast?'

'Inside one of the houses. Use your imagination. You may be devoid of talent but no one can deny that you do have that.'

'If you are going to be rude–'

'Persevere, Katie. Resume the pose.'

Katie hoisted the lamp once more. She twisted her head to look at the screen. 'I can't see the bridegroom.'

'Be patient. He's coming now.'

'If you think that is amusing…'

'I do.' Vyse stooped down and picked an object out of a holdall in the corner and came over to where she was standing.

'What is that in your hand?' she asked nervously, edging away from him.

'A light meter. Now, don't run away. It won't bite you.'

'Why do you have to hold it so close?'

'To get a proper reading.'

'Why can't you keep it still? Why does it have to go all over me?'

'Because your hair is dark. That gives me one reading. Your shoulders reflect a lot of light. That gives me another. Your breasts–'

'I get the idea. Just hurry up.'

'Relax. Just forget what I am doing.'

'How can I?'

'Concentrate on holding the position. Raise the lamp higher … remember, the light is failing.'

'The marriage took place at midnight. In case you have forgotten.'

'Don't quibble. Now, look up … that's charming…' He crouched down behind the camera, adjusted the settings, then there was a flash, a second, a third. As he straightened he passed a hand over his eyes. 'I don't know what's come over me. I feel distinctly groggy.'

'Do you want to go and lie down?'

He widened his eyes at her. 'That's my line, darling – not yours. No, I will go and get a glass of water. I will be better in a moment.'

A few minutes later, he returned shaking his head. 'I shall take your advice … stretch out on my bed for a short nap.'

'Have you finished photographing?'

'N o . I want a couple more shots. Run around the studio for a minute or two. Imagine you are Joan of Arc at the head of her troops.'

'She didn't cavort about the countryside stark naked.'

'Well, you can be Lady Godiva riding into Coventry…' his voice trailed off as he disappeared in the direction of the bedroom.

Katie cantered around the room kicking up her heels. She was in a warm, dazzling limbo. The hot brilliance of the lights seemed to have banished the dimensions of time and distance. It must be like arriving in heaven.

If Henry only knew at what sacrifice his future happiness had been secured. But Henry should never know. The secret would be interred deep down in her unmendable heart. For a moment she had quite forgotten about Lady Godiva. She slowed to a high-stepping trot. Tossing her long hair about her head, she gave a little neigh.

The curtains parted. A young woman in a dark-blue tailored dress was staring at her. Her arms were bare and the colour of pale honey. She wore three silver bracelets above the elbow. On her feet were blue and white strappy high-heel sandals. Her hair hugged her head like a golden helmet.

'Who are you?' the woman demanded.

Katie gaped at her. 'Katie … Katie Colville. Who are you?'

'Lorna. Lorna Baillie.'

'How did you get in?'

'With a key.' She held it up before slipping it into her shoulder bag. 'It used to go with the job.' Her eyes narrowed as she frowned. 'Aren't you a friend of Henry Rawnsley?'

'Yes … that is to say, my home … I mean my parents live quite close to Trystan Hall.' Katie crossed her legs, locking her feet together at the ankles, wrapping her arms about her upper parts.

Lorna Baillie regarded the contortions with curiosity. 'My fiancé has mentioned you. He said that you were a nice, quiet country girl who liked dogs and horses but you seem to be shedding the homespun image.'

'It's not what it looks like.'

'I'm not quite sure what it does look like. Are you trying to turn yourself into a corkscrew? Go on like that and you will probably sink through the floor.'

'If only I could.'

Lorna gave a shrug of indifference. 'Where's Gerald?'

'In the bedroom. I expected him back by now. I haven't been in there.'

'Just getting in the mood, were you? I won't delay you more than a few minutes. Gerald has some old negatives that belong to me. He has been rather dilatory in returning them.'

'Let me come with you. My … my knickers are somewhere here–'

'Don't bother on my account. If I had known there was a big scene here tonight, I wouldn't have barged in.'

'Lorna – believe me – there was no big scene … nothing happened here tonight…'

Lorna went on ahead. She picked up Katie's knickers and, a few paces further on, her bra and handed them to their owner with a wordless lift of her eyebrows.

They stared at the prone figure on the bed. Lorna bent over him. 'What did you do to Gerald? He seems to have passed out.'

'I swear I didn't do anything to him … I mean with him…'

Lorna laid a hand on his forehead and turned to Katie. 'He is getting on for forty, you know,' she said sternly. 'Just because Gerald has a certain reputation, girls like you see him as some sort of a challenge. You put on a Strauss tape, the 'Pizzicato Polka' or something frantic like that, wind him up like an overstrung piano and when he's given his all, push him for an encore. It isn't fair.'

'It was nothing like that. Listen to me, Lorna–'

'So it wasn't Strauss?'

'For a start, Gerald chose the music, an old Louis Armstrong number. Very slow but–'

'Not slow enough by the look of him.'

'If you must know, I gave him two sleeping pills. I put them in his brandy when he wasn't looking.'

'You came here and gave Gerald sleeping pills? Surely you mean pep pills?'

'No, it was Temazepam. They are rather strong. I was afraid he would get out of hand.'

'If you didn't want him to get out of hand, what are you doing running around his flat with no clothes on?'

'I have been trying to tell you if only you would listen.'

'I haven't time now. Do you know where he keeps his keys?'

'They are probably on him.'

Lorna put her hand in a pocket of his dressing gown. 'I have them.' She slid the keys around the ring.

Katie pulled on her knickers and fastened her bra. 'Those negatives will probably be in the safe.'

'So Gerald showed you the safe. That was a mark of great favour.'

'Let me show you.'

'I know my way around. You are the new girl here. I graduated some time ago.' Lorna led the way back to the sitting room. Reaching up, she removed the picture from over the fireplace, selected a key, pulled open the door and took out a box of transparencies.

'There's a package inside which Gerald–'

'Do shut up. I want to find my negatives.' She perched on the arm of a chair by the fire and holding up the transparencies to the lamplight, examined them one by one. 'Here's one of Libby Hayhoe wearing a dog harness. Very bizarre. Do you know Libby?'

'I don't think so.'

'She married a captain in the Brigade.'

'May I see?'

'Certainly not. Here's another odd one. Adele Carteret sitting in a laundry basket and drinking out of a coconut.' Lorna retrieved her property and dropped the negatives into her bag.

'Lorna, may I ask you something?'

'Yes. But I don't promise to give you an answer.'

'What does Gerald want from a woman? A circus performance in the bedroom? A different act every night? A woman has so much to give a man – love, loyalty–'

'To Gerald that's like one brand of Heinz soup. It's not enough. He wants the fifty-seven varieties. No one woman can provide that.'

Katie cast about for her stockings. 'I think I shall become a nun.'

'Don't tell Gerald. He will want to create a whole new scene around that idea.'

'What are you two doing rifling my safe?' Vyse barked at them from the doorway.

'I am merely taking what is mine,' Lorna replied coolly. She offered her cheek for a kiss.

Vyse crossed the room to where she was standing and kissed her. His eyes were smudged with fatigue. 'Did I hear you say that you were going to become a nun?'

'No, that was Katie.'

'Katie will have to learn to dress a little more conservatively before she goes to see the Mother Superior.' He bent down and picked up the girl's shift and gave it to her.

Katie followed his eyes as they travelled from his keys on the mantelpiece to the open safe. She placed a hand on Lorna's arm. 'Before Gerald locks that safe, there's something you ought to know.'

'Yes, Lorna,' said Gerald testily. 'Take your wedding present and let's all get off to bed.'

Lorna reached into the safe and took out the parcel. 'Not a very gracious speech but I may forgive you if I like my picture.'

'I have never done anything better. You look exquisite.'

Katie stared from one to the other, her eyes as large as satellite dishes. 'Lorna …' she cleared her throat of some obstruction, 'do you know what is in that parcel?'

'Of course I do. It's my bridal photograph … or Gerald's version of it.'

'You in church wearing … wearing practically nothing,' said Katie, her voice on a precarious note. She struggled into her shift. 'I could tell you what I think about photographs like that. And what I think about sending such a thing to the picture framers for those two freaks to slaver over but … but you would say I was a sanctimonious little prig.' Her face was scarlet, her eyes bright with unshed tears. '*I don't understand the world that you two live in,*' she cried, 'and what is more, I don't want to understand it.'

'*Gerald!* You didn't send my photograph to the framers!' Lorna glowered at him. 'It was private. Something between the two of us. How dare you hawk my picture round the local tradesmen!'

'It's worse than that, Lorna. Gerald told them that he was going to send it to Henry Rawnsley.'

Lorna gripped Gerald's arm. 'Is that true, Gerald? What a four-letter man you are.'

Vyse raised his hands in surrender. 'It was just a joke. How did I know that Malcolm would take it seriously? He should have known that no gentleman–'

'How he could mistake you for a gentleman I cannot imagine. Were you showing off, Gerald? Or was it spite? Were you getting back at me? Or did you hope that if you fed them a spicy morsel of tittle-tattle, you might get the framing done free?'

'Who knows?' Vyse spread his hands wearily. 'I'm sorry but it was one of those bad days. I was lonely.

And out of love … it always brings out the worst in me.'

'That courier…' Katie began. Her mouth opened and closed as she tried to form the words.

'There's no point in him coming now. I was going to send him away.' Vyse went to the telephone and dialled a number. He spoke a few words and replaced the receiver.

Lorna turned a puzzled face on her companions. 'What was the courier for?'

'It's a secret between Katie and me,' Vyse replied. He put the transparencies back in the safe, locked it and swung the picture into position once more. He cast a sidelong glance at Katie.

Katie had fought to hold back the tears but her resistance had been worn down. The banks of the stream gave way. 'Gerald ordered a courier … to make me think that Lorna's photograph was being sent to Henry … that's why I took my clothes off … poor, darling Henry … he is such a romantic … it would have spoiled everything … he would have broken off the engagement . . . never married … become old and miserable and lonely…'

'Join the club,' said Vyse with an attempt at flippancy which sounded strangely off key.

Katie turned her red-rimmed eyes on Vyse. 'How could you do it, Gerald? Make me undress … before a complete stranger … a man I never even knew existed before today …wearing nothing … not even a straw hat … and carrying a … a hurricane lamp.' She buried her face in her hands.

Lorna took Katie in her arms. 'You mustn't cry. Don't give a man the satisfaction of thinking he has got the better of you.' She found a tissue and mopped the girl's eyes.

Katie snuffled, wrinkling her nose disdainfully at Vyse who was poking morosely among the embers of the fire. 'Promise me, Lorna, that you won't let Henry see that photograph of you.'

'Not even when we are married?' Lorna gave Katie a kiss and zipped her into her dress.

'Henry is very sweet but he is rather an innocent.' Katie found a handkerchief and blew her nose. 'And I do want him to be happy.'

'Then I will hide it away. It will be my first secret from poor, darling Henry.'

'Don't say "poor, darling Henry" like that. You make him sound so feeble, so ineffectual. He's not like that at all.'

'Of course he is not. I wouldn't be marrying him if I thought so. It was a joke, that's all.'

Katie shook her head. 'I seem to have missed all the jokes tonight. You must think me very dreary.' She picked up her bag and looked about the room forlornly. Her fingers trailed along the arm of a chair. 'Lorna has got what she came for,' she said in a flat voice. 'And Gerald must be quite elated, like a burglar after a successful evening's work.'

Vyse raised his eyebrows in surprise. 'What have I stolen from you?'

'Something that belonged to me,' Katie replied in a low voice. 'Something I wasn't ready to share.'

Vyse turned off the table lamp. 'You escaped lightly. You still have the apple. All I got was the peel. Rather green and a little too sour for my taste.'

'Call a truce, you two,' said Lorna. 'I'm going home.'

Katie pushed her feet into her shoes. 'I wonder who will be here tomorrow night,' she mused, half to herself. 'I wonder what role she will be made to play. I wonder what cage of props and gadgets and devices Gerald will build around her so that she can never get too close to him.'

Lorna's hand went to the zip on her shoulder bag. 'I have the key to my cage, Gerald. You can have it back.'

'Are you sure you won't still need it?'

'Quite sure. You must find another captive.'

Vyse took the key and dangled it from its chain, watching it swing slowly from side to side like a pendulum. 'I, too, wonder who will be here tomorrow night,' he murmured. His dark eyes turned to Katie. 'It would be sad to go away empty-handed.' He held up the key somewhat tentatively between finger and thumb. 'What do you say, Katie?'

In Brief

Charles Owen writes the Army obituaries for the Daily Telegraph. He has been variously a stockbroker, a merchant banker, a cavalry officer, a Ministry of Defence contractor and an engineering export salesman. *Cry Cassandra*! and *Fiamma* were published recently. Four collections of short stories – *A Crack in the Glass, The Mark of the Beast, Man Overboard* and *Escapade* – are now being published simultaneously.

Meet the Author, Charles Owen

I was born in 1935. When the Second World War broke out a few years later, I was shipped off from a Devonshire hill farm to Australia. My father, who was wounded in the First World War, was then in MI5. He believed that the Germans might invade and probably wanted my mother, sister and myself out of the way.

In 1942, we were returning to England when we were torpedoed by a German submarine in the North Atlantic. The ship was sent to the bottom but after taking to the waves in a lifeboat we were all rescued by the US Navy.

Aged 12, I went to Eton. Top hats were being phased out. They were routinely maltreated until the boys wearing them looked like something out of the music hall. But if the school was slowly changing, the house where I boarded lacked all mod cons and was later pulled down.

In 1956, in my first term at Cambridge and despite the objections of the Foreign Office, I set off to Budapest in the hope of helping the Hungarians in their revolution against the Soviets. My involvement made little difference to the outcome of that tragic affair but the experience provided the inspiration for my forthcoming book, *The Dido Decrypt.*

I did my National Service with a cavalry regiment in Germany. Our job was to discourage the Red Army from crossing the Rhine. As a tank commander, it was wise to keep well in with your driver. If he was cross with you, he would give you a bumpy ride which would loosen every tooth in your head.

A spell in stock-broking and merchant banking persuaded me that I was better at making things than making money and there followed many productive years as the export director of an engineering company. We were contractors to the Ministry of Defence and there was a lot of travelling to the Middle East. The work was absorbing, exacting and, sometimes, frightening.

In 2000, for the Daily Telegraph, I began writing up the stories of the surviving men and women who had been awarded the Victoria Cross or the George Cross. That led to writing the obituaries of those who had had adventurous and distinguished careers in the British Army. To date, several hundred of these can be read on the internet.

In the course of reading private papers and unpublished memoirs that have passed through my hands, I became fascinated by the exciting and often perilous careers of servicemen and women who were involved in Intelligence operations; spies and counter-spies, secret agents and members of the Special Operations Executive who were parachuted into enemy-occupied countries to train and arm the Resistance. *The Voce Vendetta*, relating the fictional exploits of Captain Rohan Voce, will be published in 2016 and will, I hope, bring an account of some of these clandestine operations to a wider readership.

Acknowledgements

My heartfelt thanks go to Georgie, my daughter, who helped to unravel the seemingly impenetrable mysteries of the word processor, also to my son, Jamie, whose guidance has proved invaluable in my wanderings through the trackless wastes of journalism; and to Pierre, my brother-in-law, whose expertise, unstintingly shared, kept my spirits up and my blood pressure down when the hardware and software sulked or threatened to mutiny. I have nothing but praise for the unwinking editorial eyes of the proof-readers. Rosie, heroically volunteered to give the manuscript a final vetting. Any errors that remain are my responsibility.